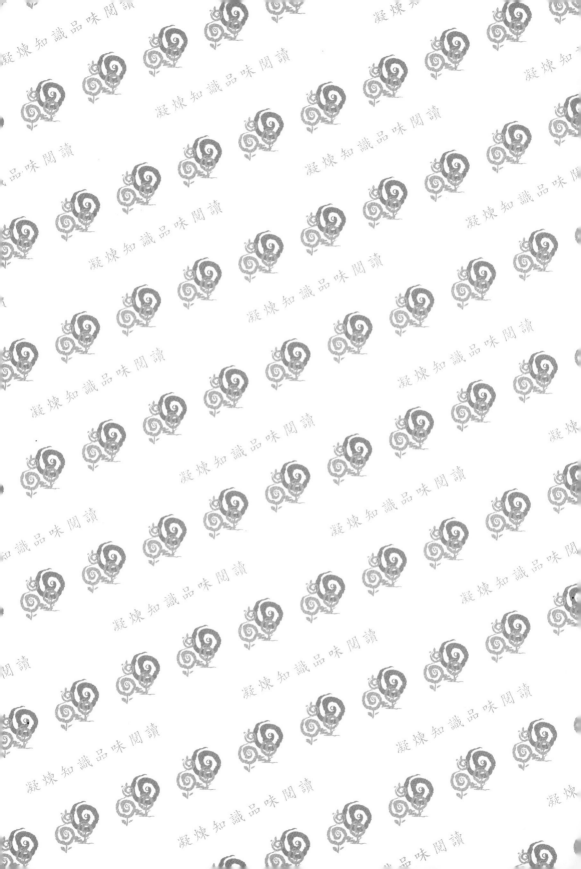

華 健 編著

輪機英文
English for Marine Engineer

五南圖書出版公司 印行

序

　　英文對於一位輪機員的重要性無須贅述。但真正的問題，在於如何實際有效的提升輪機員使用英文的能力。依作者的經驗，任何實用性語言皆如同我們手上的工具，在對的基礎上反覆運用，便自然得心應手，且能夠嚐出箇中趣味。只不過身為輪機員，往往動手機會多，動口機會少，以致英語疏於練習，用時方恨少。因此在本書當中，作者一再提醒讀者的是「先讀為快」策略，不僅要養成面對任何英文便信口「Read out」的習慣，而且最好是能在情況允許時「Read out loud」。

　　相信照這樣繼續讀下去，不久，您對輪機英文，便可在趣味中建立信心，在信心下培養出趣味。這本書以「閱讀輪機」作為開頭，加上「口說輪機」和「輪機文書」，共三大部分。讀者在書中會發現不少字都會出現不一致的拼法，例如：「Sulphur」與「Sulfur」、「Vapor」與「Vapour」、「Organized」與「Organised」等，這些不外是英式與美式拼法的差別，在現實場合當中便是如此，都算對，也都好用。由衷希望這本書能為讀者在接下來的輪機生涯當中幫上忙。

目錄

第三章　輪機文書（Writing Marine Engineering）　105

第四章　測驗例題　159

參考文獻（References）　171

附錄　175

002

第一章　閱讀輪機
（Read Marine Engineering）

第一節　認識船

　　在輪機員的生涯當中，無論是為了在工作中勝任愉快，或是持續學習以更上層樓，皆需要閱讀大量的專業文章。這些文章有些是船上或公司提供的，有些則是自己透過各種管道蒐集來的，不難預期，絕大部分都是英文。因此，培養閱讀英文文章的習慣，對一個輪機員而言，是最不可或缺的。本章整理了一些輪機專業相關短文，目的在引導讀者培養這方面的興趣與能力。我們就從下圖所示，船上各部位與設備的名稱開始吧！

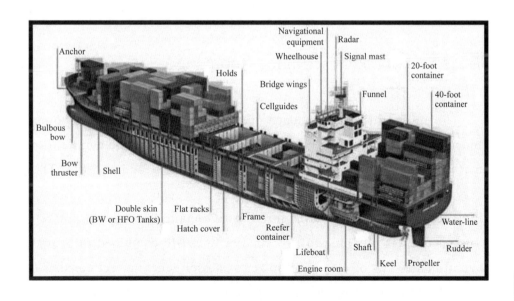

Anchor	錨	Holds	貨艙
Bulbous bow	球型艏	Keel	龍骨
Bow thruster	艏推進器	Reefer container	冷凍冷藏貨櫃
Bridge wings	船橋翼	Navigational equipment	航行儀器設備
Cellguides	艙內導軌	Radar	雷達
Double skin	雙重殼	Signal mast	信號樟桿
Engine room	機艙	Rudder	舵
40-foot container	40呎長貨櫃	Propeller	推進器、螺槳
Flat racks	平架	20-foot container	20呎貨櫃
Frame	結構肋板	Water-line	吃水線
Hatch cover	貨艙蓋		

接下來，我們先到機艙（Engine room）看看。請暫時不急著查字典，先盡量反覆熟讀這篇短文，再想想它們究竟是什麼意思，持續努力，養成「先讀為快」的習慣！

第二節　認識機艙（Engine Room）

The engine room is the space on the ship where almost all the machinery is located. Several equipmentarelocated outside the engine room such as anchor windlass, propeller, cranes, winches, and so forth. They are so categorized as deck machineries.

The engine room contains three to five main diesel generator sets. These main sets plus one to two smaller ones are combined to provide several megawatts of electrical power. A diesel generator set consists of a diesel engine driving an AC generator and includes auxiliary equipment such as cooling pumps, lube oil pumps, fuel oil pumps, coolers and more.

When we come down to middle and bottom platform of the engine room there are various types and uses of pumps including fire pumps, general service pumps, sea water cooling pumps, ballast pumps, fuel oil transfer pumps, lubricating oil transfer pumps, bilge pumps, sludge pumps, air conditioner condenser pumps, fridge pumps, fire and general service pump, piston cooling water pump, and jacket cooling water pumps.

There are different kinds of tanks meant for storage of various liquids. They are for example, fuel oil drain tank, sludge drain tank, lube oil drain tank, stuffing oil drain tank, and bilge holding tank. To avoid the mixing of two different liquids a void space is provided between two tanks. This prevents any accidental intermixing of two different liquids due to leaking.

The engine control room (ECR) is directly above main machinery spaces. The ECR has a console that houses operator stations for the centralized system used to monitor and control the ship's machinery throughout the vessel. It also houses the main switchboard and the ship's service switchboard for control and distribution of the electricity used onboard. The ECR also serves as an office for Engine Department personnel where technical manuals, drawings and files are kept, as well as computers for management software programs. Marine Engineers use the ECR as a base of operations, and for work, planning, and safety meetings.

讀了上面這段，讀者可能發現，分析文章當中的每個字彙，真正稱得上是生字的沒幾個，但卻又不怎麼了解通篇文章的意思。這主要可能是對機艙的實際狀況還生疏，或者是個人在輪機專業和英語之間，少了一些銜接的橋梁。解決之道在於，若屬於前者的情形，須持續學習輪機專業領域；若屬後者，則須努力銜接英語和輪機。而無論屬於何者，共同最可行且有效的方法，莫過於培養開口熟讀。所接觸到的各種輪機相關文章，由短而長、從淺到深，只要願意持續讀下去，便會逐漸讀出味道、讀出心得，進而真正享受到學習的樂趣和成就感。

第三節　輪機資訊

　　本章接下來整理一些與輪機專業密切相關的短文，供讀者練習。文章當中以斜體字標出較有可能需要解釋的字與詞，便利讀者查閱。請反覆朗誦以下短文，同時想想句中的意思。

一、引擎出力與油耗（Engine Power Range and Fuel Oil Consumption）

　　一艘船的油耗率和制動馬力（Brake horsepower, BHP）與以下參數有關，例如：

1. 進氣溫度　　Blower inlet temperature　　　25°C
2. 進氣壓力　　Blower inlet pressure　　　　 1,000 mbar
3. 燃油低熱值　Fuel oil lower calorific value　 42,700 kJ/kg
　　　　　　　　　　　　　　　　　　　　　　（~10,200 kCal/kg）

二、燃油消耗率（Specific Fuel Oil Consumption）

　　The specific fuel oil consumption (SFOC) is guaranteed for one engine load (power-speed combination), this being the one in which the engine is optimized. The *cylinder oil* consumption *figures* are valid under normal conditions. During running periods and under special conditions, feed rates of up to 1.5 times the stated values should be used.

Cylinder oil	氣缸潤滑油	**Figures**	數值

三、柴油發電機（Diesel Generator）

When a diesel engine drives the *armature* to goes round quickly between *magnets*, electricity flows through the armature wires to the *commutator* and *carbon brushes*. 450 Volts of power goes to the *control panel* to *distribute* electricity to power equipments onboard ship.

Armature	電樞	**Carbon brushes**	碳刷
Magnets	磁鐵	**Control panel**	配電盤
Commutator	整流子	**Distribute**	配送

四、推進系統的選擇（Selection of Propulsion System）

Diesel propulsion for commercial oceangoing ships is primarily low-speed diesel engines (RPM less than 400) and medium-speed diesel engines (RPM 400 to 1,400). Smaller ships, tugs, ferries and high-speed craft can have high-speed diesel engines (RPM over 1,400).

There are many reasons for selection of a specific propulsion system for a particular ship, including the size of the ship, its power relative to its draft, how many propellers are fitted, special *manoeuvrability* requirements, special *operating profiles* and others.

Where fuel efficiency is the primary goal low-speed diesel engines would be the first choice since they have the lowest *specific fuel oil consumption* (SFOC) of the diesel engine choices. For low-speed diesel engines, fuel efficiency can reach up to 55 percent in the current state of technology. This means more than half the energy content of the fuel is converted to mechanical energy by the low-speed diesel engine and can be *directly transmitted* to the propeller.

Medium-speed diesel engines have slightly higher SFOC, which means that their efficiency is slightly lower, usually about 3 to 4 percent lower at similar power levels. Medium-speed engines must be connected to the propeller through a *speed reducing transmission system* – either a *reduction gear* or an electric drive system. When connected to the propeller through a gearbox there is about a 2 percent loss in power delivered to the propeller. When connected to the propeller through an electric drive system there is about a 10 percent loss in power delivered to the propeller.

Considering the losses in power transmission means that for the same propeller power, medium-speed diesel engines must develop about 2 percent more power in the *geared design*, and about 11 percent more in the *electric drive design*. This increase in required power coupled with the higher SFOC for medium-speed diesel engines may result in increased fuel consumption over the low-speed diesel for the same power at design condition and propeller RPM.

Manoeuvrability	操控性	Speed reducing transmission system	減速傳遞系統
Operating profiles	運轉概況	Reduction gear	減速齒輪
Specific fuel oil consumption	燃油油耗率	Geared design	齒輪驅動設計
Directly transmitted	直接傳遞	Electric drive design	電動設計

五、汽機船的機艙（Engine Room of Steam Ship (S.S.)）

　　前面我們談的是在以柴油引擎為推進動力的「油機船」（Motor ship/Motor vessel, MS/MV）機艙的情形，以下我們來看看「汽機船」的機艙。如今只有在很偶然的機會才會遇到蒸汽機船。請對照下圖當中的標號，朗讀以下這段短文。

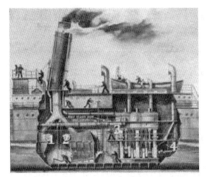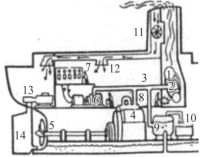

蒸汽機船的機艙

1. Boiler and

2. superheater turn water to superheated steam.

3. The steam goes to

4. drive propeller turbines which drive

5. the propeller shaft and blades.

6. Superheated stem also used to drives the turbo-generator, which gen-

erates electricity and send it to

7. all parts of the ship through a control panel.

8. Steam can also be used to heat sea water and to generate fresh water.

9. The sea water boils and gives off steam, which

10. cools into drops of fresh water.

11. A draft blower sends fresh air to the ventilation system.

12. The steering gear which is a push-pull motor turns

13. the rudder to control ship direction.

六、艙底水系統 （Bilge System）

Waste water drains to the ship's bottom – the bilge. It is then pumped routinely through an *oily water separator* (OWS) and *overboard* by the bilge pump. The OWS is used to treat the oily bilge water to be less than the internationally regulated limit of 15 part per million (ppm).

Oily water separator	油水分離器	Overboard	船外

七、排氣旁通 （Exhaust Gas by-pass）

Compensation for low *ambient temperature* can be obtained by using exhaust gas by-pass system. This arrangement ensures that only part of the exhaust gas goes via the turbine of the turbocharger, thus supplying less energy to the compressor which, in turn, reduces the air supply to the engine.

Compensation	彌補	Ambient temperature	外界溫度

八、緊急運轉狀況（Emergency Running Condition）

By-pass of the total amount of exhaust gas around the turbocharger (*T/C*) is only used for emergency running (shown in figure below) in the event of turbocharger failure on engines. This enables the engine to run at a higher load with only one turbocharger under emergency conditions. The engine's *exhaust gas receiver* will in this case be fitted with a by-pass flange of approximately the same diameter as the inlet pipe to the turbocharger.

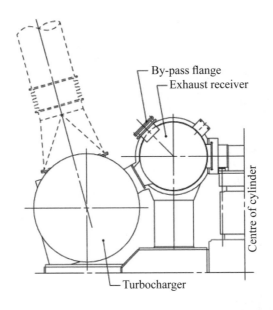

T/C	過給氣機，排氣增壓機
Exhaust gas receiver	排氣接收器

九、掃氣系統（Scavenge Air System）

Scavenge air is supplied to the engine by one or two turbochargers located on the exhaust side of the engine, or from one turbocharger located on the aft end of the engine, option. The compressor of the turbocharger draws air from the engine room, through an *air filter*, and the *compressed air* is cooled by the scavenge air cooler. The *scavenge air cooler* is provided with a *water mist catcher*, which prevents condensed water from being carried with the air into the scavenge air receiver and to the *combustion chamber*.

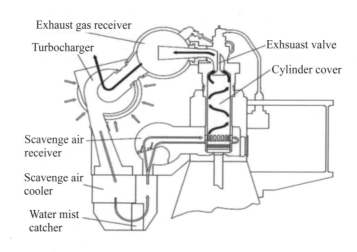

Exhaust gas receiver
Turbocharger
Exhsuast valve
Cylinder cover
Scavenge air receiver
Scavenge air cooler
Water mist catcher

Air filter	空氣濾清器	Compressed air	壓縮空氣
Scavenge air cooler	掃氣冷卻器	Water mist catcher	水霧收集器
Combustion chamber	燃燒室		

十、極端天候狀況（Extreme Ambient Conditions）

Marine diesel engines are exposed to greatly varying climatic temperatures winter and summer in *arctic* as well as tropical areas. These variations cause changes of the *scavenge air* pressure, the maximum combustion pressure, the exhaust gas amount and temperatures as well as the specific fuel oil consumption. For air inlet temperatures below 10°C the *precautions* to be taken depend very much on the *operating profile* of the vessel.

Arctic	北極	Precautions	警覺
Scavenge air	掃氣	Operating profile	運轉輪廓

十一、發電柴油引擎（Generator Diesel Engine）

Electric power may be developed aboard ship by a generator attached to the main propulsion engine or by generators driven by independent diesel engines. Whether or not the ship has a main engine-driven generator, it will still require additional generators that are normally driven by medium-speed or in some cases high-speed, diesel engines. Generators for AC power are driven at a constant speed that is found by dividing 7,200 (for 60 Hz) or 6,000 (for 50 Hz) by the number of poles (only an even number of poles are used). The larger the number of poles, results in slower generator RPM and higher costs.

Large *auxiliary engines* driving generators for electric drive ships typically operate at about 500 RPM (12 poles/50 Hz). Diesel engines providing power for ship service generators would typically have speeds between 720 and 1,000 RPM, depending on the AC frequency selected.

With the advent of reliable *microprocessors* and computer controls, it is now possible to *electronically control* the *fuel injection timing*, fuel injection quantity and, on low-speed diesel engines, exhaust valve timing. This changes the traditional *camshaft-driven* fuel injection pumps and valve *hydraulic pumps* to high pressure *common rails* with *solenoid valves* that are opened and closed by the electronic control system. The key to the functioning of the electronically controlled engine is the *servo hydraulic system* which powers exhaust valve operation and the fuel injection pumps. The fuel is pumped up to high pressure and distributed to the fuel injector pipes by a *fuel main* running along the side of the engine.

Auxiliary engines	輔引擎	Hydraulic pumps	油壓泵
Microprocessors	微處理器	Common rails	共軌
Electronically control	電子控制	Solenoid valves	電磁閥
Fuel injection timing	噴油正時	Servo hydraulic system	伺服液壓系統
Camshaft-driven	由曲拐軸驅動	Fuel main	燃油總管

十二、船用引擎的過給氣機 （Turbocharger for Marine Diesel Engine）

By *turbocharging* an engine, the following advantages are obtained.

- It increases power for an engine of the same size or reduction in size for an engine with the same power output.

- It reduces specific fuel oil consumption. Mechanical, thermal and scavenge efficiencies are therefore improved due to greater air supply and use of exhaust gasses.

- It reduces thermal loading due to shorter but more efficient burning period for the fuel.

The turbocharger consists of a single stage *impulse turbine* connected to a *centrifugal impeller* via a shaft (following figures). On the turbine side the turbine is driven by the engine exhaust gas, which enters via the gas inlet casing. The gas expands through a *nozzle ring* where the pressure energy of the gas is converted to kinetic energy. This high velocity gas is directed onto the turbine blades where it drives the turbine wheel, and thus the compressor at high speeds (up to 15,000 RPM). The exhaust gas then passes through the outlet casing to the *exhaust uptakes*.

Turbocharging	渦輪增壓	Impulse turbine	衝動渦機輪
Nozzle ring	噴嘴圓環	Centrifugal impeller	離心葉輪
Exhaust uptakes	排氣吸口		

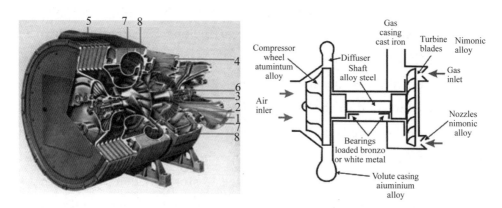

圖中編號	名稱	圖中編號	名稱
1	Gas inlet casing	5	Silencer filter
2	Turbine nozzle	6	Compressor
3	Turbine wheel	7	Diffuser
4	Gas outlet casing	8	Volute casing

On the *blower side* air is drawn in through sponge-like filters, and enters the compressor wheel axially where it is accelerated to high velocity. The air exits the impeller *radially* and passes through a *diffuser*, where some of the kinetic energy gets converted to pressure energy. The air passes to the *volute casing* where a further energy conversion takes place.

Blower side	鼓風側	Diffuser	擴散口
Radially	徑向的	Volute casing	渦卷式機殼

十三、引擎如何靠空氣啟動（How an Engine Starts on Air）

Large marine diesel engines are started using high pressure air. The air is admitted into the cylinder when the piston is just past top dead center (TDC) and continued until just before the exhaust valve opens. There is always more than one air start valve open: a situation known as overlap. This ensures that the engine will start in any position.

The opening of the main air start valves is controlled by a set of *pilot valves* located in the *air start distributor*, which in turn are timed to operate by a drive linked to the main camshaft. Figure below shows a small camshaft is used to control the opening and closing of the air start pilot valves. Large air receivers are used to store the compressed air. As shown in the Figure, the isolating valve open so air is being allowed as far as the automatic valve and the air start control valve.

When the engine is required to start, a low pressure air signal is sent to the air start control valve (which can also be hand operated in an emergency). The air pushes a piston down which opens the valve and allows high pressure air to flow to the pilot valve and the automatic valve operating pistons. The pilot valve is forced down onto the cam profile and the automatic valve opens and high pressure air is led to the main air start valves and the pilot valve. When the pilot valve *cam follower* is on the lowest point on the cam, air flows to the operating piston of the main air start valve for that particular cylinder, opens the valve and allows high pressure air to flow into the cylinder.

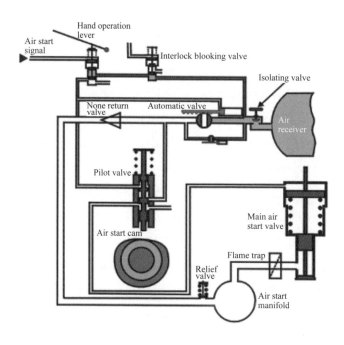

Pilot valves	導閥	Cam follower	凸輪從動器
Air start distributor	空氣啟動分配器		

十四、海運燃料（Marine Fuels）

Heavy fuel oils (HFO) are used widely in marine applications in combustion equipment such as main engines, auxiliary engines and boilers. They are blended products based on the residues from refinery *distillation* and *cracking* processes. Due to the progress in refining technology, the process becoming more sophisticated to extract higher value fuels.

Different hydrocarbon structures' chain lengths have progressively higher boiling points, so they can all be separated by distillation. Crude oil is heated and the different chains are separated out by their differing vaporization temperatures.

The oldest and most common way to separate crude oil into the various components (called fractions), is to use the differences in *boiling point* (BP). This process is called *fractional distillation*. Crude oil is heated, vaporized and then the vapor is condensed. Newer techniques use chemical processing on some of the fractions to make others, in a process called *conversion*.

HFO is a general term, and other names commonly used to describe this range of products include: *residual fuel oil* (RFO), bunker fuel (BF), bunker C, fuel oil No. 6, industrial fuel oil, marine fuel oil (MFO) and black oil. In addition, terms such as HFO, intermediate fuel oil (IFO) and light fuel oil (LFO) are also used to describe products for industrial applications, to give a general indication of the viscosity and density of the product.

As a residual product, HFO is a relatively inexpensive fuel – typically its costs around 30% less than distillate fuels. It has become the standard fuel for large, slow speed marine diesel engines, this being especially so during the oil crises of the 1970s and 1980s. Its use required extensive research and development of the fuel injection system and other components of low and medium speed engines.

With the high cost of fuel and the regulatory efforts to reduce harmful emissions it is important that the engines operate in as efficient a manner as practical. *Enhanced efficiency* can be achieved via new equipment and systems or by improved operating procedures. In order to monitor how efficiently the engines are operating, and to see the effects of changes in operating procedures, it is necessary to have the right equipment installed to monitor both power output and fuel consumption.

Distillation	蒸餾	Conversion	轉化
Cracking	裂解	Residual fuel oil	殘餾燃料油、渣油
Boiling point	沸點、氣化溫度	Enhanced efficiency	提升效率
Fractional distillation	分餾		

十五、氣缸潤滑（Cylinder Lubrication）

Low-speed diesel engines require cylinder oil fed into the cylinder liners to provide lubrication of the cylinder walls and to *neutralize* the *corrosive effects* of acids in the *combustion chamber* formed from the *sulphur content* of the fuel.

Traditionally this lubrication was provided by mechanical systems with individual camshaft driven piston pumps feeding *lubricating quills* installed around each cylinder liner. The engine makers now offer electronically controlled cylinder lubrication systems that inject controlled amounts of cylinder oil from a common high pressure oil pipe that feeds individual lubricators.

The injection of the cylinder oil from the lubricators to each lubricating quill is controlled by *solenoid valves*. The quantity of oil and the timing of the injection are electronically controlled and are varied depending on engine load and can be adjusted to suit the sulphur content of the fuel.

For electronically controlled engines special exhaust gas and turbocharger control equipment can be installed on some low-speed diesel engines that will reduce SFOC at low to medium loads. This can be important for ships that will be *operating consistently* at less than full speed to achieve lower fuel consumption or to *suit service requirements*. To achieve this reduction requires special turbochargers. The system can be tuned for *partial load operation* (65 to 85 percent *maximum continu-ous rating*, MCR) or low load operation (about 50 to 65 percent MCR).

Variable Turbocharger Area (VTA for MAN) and *Variable Turbine Geometry* (VTG for Wärtsilä) – This method is available for large-bore modern two-stroke and four-stroke diesel engines, as well as for gas engines. The area of the *nozzle ring* of the turbochargers is varied depending on the load. It requires special turbo charger parts be installed. The nozzle ring area is maximized when at full load and is decreased as engine load is reduced to a minimum at a designated engine load depending on the optimization point.

Neutralize	中和	Suit service requirements	適應運轉要求
Corrosive effects	腐蝕效果	Partial load operation	部分負荷運轉
Combustion chamber	燃燒室	Maximum continuous rating	最大連續額定值
Sulphur content	含硫量	Variable turbocharger area	可變截面渦輪增壓機
Lubricating quills	潤滑滾針	Variable turbine geometry	可變幾何特性增壓機
Solenoid valves	電磁閥	Nozzle ring	噴嘴環
Operating consistently	持續運轉		

十六、海水冷卻（Seawater Cooling）

The number of pumps, compressors and other items of equipment installed are determined by *classification society*, IMO and *flag State* requirements, based on the need for *redundancy* in case of failure of a running unit, and to provide *operational flexibility*. Unit size/capacity and the number of units installed are selected to meet the most *severe* design conditions. For example, often three sea water cooling pumps are provided, each rated for 50 percent of the maximum sea water demand when the sea water is at the maximum design temperature.

Often in service, the sea water temperature is significantly below the maximum design temperature, some cooling loads are not in operation, heat exchangers may not be *fouled to the extent* assumed in their design specifications, and the main engine is operating at less than its maximum continuous rating. The result is that the system's cooling requirements may be served by only one pump, thus saving the energy required for running a second pump.

Many ships have two *central coolers* designed for 50 or 60 percent of the maximum cooling load, allowing one unit to be *secured* in less than maximum conditions. This allows the cooler to operate near design conditions of flow even though only one pump may be in service. Operators should be aware of these savings and should *endeavour to* operate only the number of units required to meet the actual demand without *sacrificing safety*. This applies to both new and *existing ships*. The installation of *dedicated* cooling pumps of lower power for use only in ports should be also considered.

Classification society	船級社	Central coolers	中央冷卻器
Flag State	掛旗國	Secured	停用
Redundancy	多餘度	Endeavour to	戮力
Operational flexibility	運轉彈性	Sacrificing safety	犧牲安全
Severe	嚴苛的	Existing ships	現成船
Fouled to the extent	污損到某程度	Dedicated	專用

十七、以選擇性觸媒還原系統降低NO_x（Engine with Selective Catalytic Reduction System）

If a reduction between 50 and 98% of NO_x is required, the Selective Catalytic Reduction (SCR) system has to be applied by adding *ammonia or urea* to the exhaust gas before it enters a *catalytic converter*. The exhaust gas must be mixed with ammonia before passing through the catalyst, and in order to encourage the chemical reaction the temperature level has to be between 300 and 400°C. During this process the NO_x is *reduced* to N_2 and water.

This means that the SCR unit has to be located before the turbocharger on two stroke engines because of their high *thermal efficiency* and thereby a relatively low exhaust gas temperature. The amount of ammonia injected into the exhaust gas is controlled by a process computer and is based on the NO_x production at different loads measured during the *test bed running*.

As the ammonia is a combustible gas, it is supplied through a *double-walled pipe* system, with appropriate *venting* and fitted with an ammonia leak detector. Figure below shows a simplified system layout of the SCR installation.

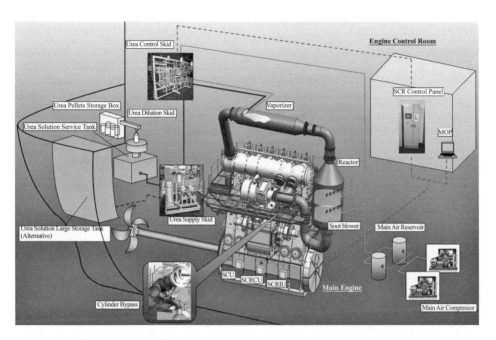

Ammonia or urea	氨／阿摩尼亞、尿素	Test bed running	試驗台運轉
Catalytic converter	觸媒轉化器	Double-walled pipe	雙層管
Reduced	還原	Venting	通氣
Thermal efficiency	熱效率		

十八、標準引擎直接接上發電機（Standard Engine with Direct Mounted Generator）

The DMG/CFE (Direct Mounted Generator/Constant Frequency Electrical) is separated from the crankcase by a plate and a *labyrinth stuffing box*. The DMG/CFE system has been developed in cooperation with the German generator manufacturers *Siemens* and *AEG*.

For generators in the normal output range, the mass of the rotor can normally be carried by the *foremost main bearing* without exceeding the permissible bearing load, but this must be checked by the engine manufacturer in each case. If the *permissible load* on the foremost main bearing is exceeded, e.g. because a *tuning wheel* is needed, this does not preclude the use of a DMG/CFE.

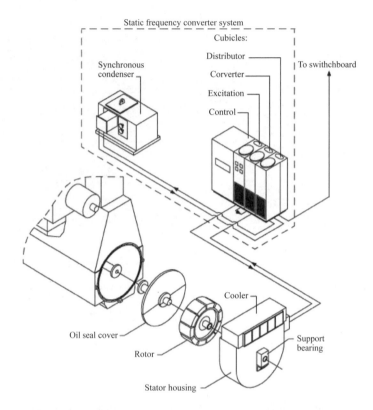

Labyrinth stuffing box	迷宮式填料函	Foremost main bearing	最重要主軸承
Siemens	西門子公司	Permissible load	容許負荷
AEG	AEG引擎公司	Tuning wheel	調整滾輪

十九、軸系接地（Shaftline Earthing (or Grounding)）

A difference in the *electrical potential* between the hull and the propeller shaft will be generated due to the difference in materials and to the propeller being immersed in sea water. In some cases, the difference in the electrical potential has caused *spark erosion* on the *thrust*, main *bearings* and *journals* of the crankshaft of the engine.

In order to reduce the electrical potential between the crankshaft and the hull and thus prevent spark erosion, a highly efficient shaftline earthing device must be installed. The shaftline earthing device should be able to keep the electrical potential difference below 50mV DC, and a *shaft-to-hull monitoring* equipment with an mV-meter and with an output signal to the alarm system must be installed so that the potential and thus the *correct function* of the shaftline earthing device can be monitored.

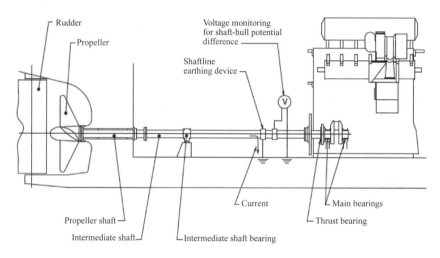

Electrical potential	電位	**Journals**	軸頸
Spark erosion	電火花侵蝕	**Shaft-to-hull monitoring**	監測軸至船殼
Thrust bearings	推力軸承	**Correct function**	正確作動

二十、氣缸滑油系統（Cylinder Lubricating Oil System）

The cost of the cylinder lubricating oil is one of the largest contributions to total *operating costs*, next to the fuel oil cost. Another aspect is that the lubrication rate has a great influence on the cylinder condition, and thus on the *overhauling schedules* and *maintenance costs*. It is therefore of the utmost importance that the cylinder lubricating oil system as well as its operation is optimized.

The cylinder lubricating oil consumption could be monitored by installing a flow meter on the pressure side of the pump in the supply line to the service tank, if required by the shipowner. Provided the oil level in the service tank is kept the same every time the flow meter is being read, the accuracy is satisfactory.

The recommendations are valid for all plants, whether *controllable* pitch or fixed *pitch propellers* are used. In case of average *sulfur content*, the average cylinder oil feed rate at *nominal* MCR for MANB&W Alpha Cylinder Lubricator is 0.7 g/kWh. The nominal cylinder oil feed rate at nominal MCR for a mechanical cylinder lubricator is typically1.5 g/kWh.

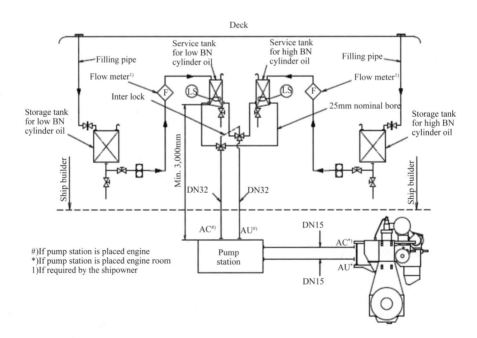

Operating costs	運轉成本	Controllable pitch propellers	可調螺距螺旋槳
Ovrhauling schedules	吊缸期程	Sulfur content	硫含量
Maintenance costs	維護成本	Nominal	公稱

二十一、中央冷卻水系統（Central Cooling Water System）

The central cooling water system is characterized by having only one heat exchanger cooled by seawater, and by the other coolers, including the *jacket water cooler*, being cooled by central cooling water. In order to prevent too high a *scavenge air temperature*, the cooling water design temperature in the central cooling water system is normally 36°C, corresponding to a maximum seawater temperature of 32°C.

The recommendation of keeping the cooling water inlet temperature to the main engine scavenge air cooler as low as possible also applies to the central cooling system. This means that the temperature control valve in the central cooling water circuit is to be set to minimum 10°C, whereby the temperature follows the outboard seawater temperature when central cooling water temperature exceeds 10°C.

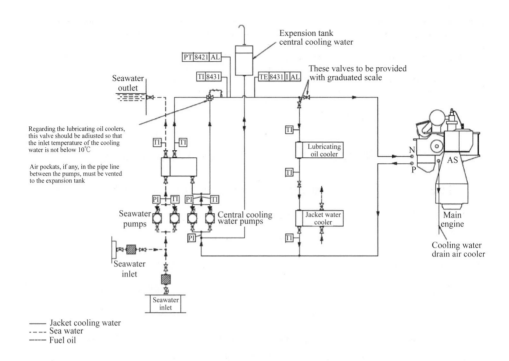

PT 8421 AL

Expension tank
central cooling water

TI 8431

These valves to be provided
with graduated scale

TE 8431 I AL

Seawater
outlet

Regarding the lubricating oil coolers,
this valve should be adjusted so that
the inlet temperature of the cooling
water is not below 10℃

Air pockats, if any, in the pipe line
between the pumps, must be vented
to the expansion tank

TI

Lubricating
oil cooler

N

AS

P

TI

TI

Seawater
pumps

PI TI PI TI

Central cooling
water pumps

Jacket water
cooler

Main
engine

Cooling water
drain air cooler

PI

Seawater
inlet

TI

Seawater
inlet

—— Jacket cooling water
---- Sea water
----- Fuel oil

Jacket water cooler	缸套水冷卻器	Scavenge air temperature	掃氣溫度

二十二、引擎控制系統（Engine Control System）

The engine is provided with a *pneumatic/electric manoeuvring* and fuel oil regulating system, which transmits *orders* from the separate *manoeuvring consoles* to the engine. By means of the regulating system it is possible to start, stop, reverse the engine and control the engine speed. The speed setting device on the manoeuvring consoles gives a speed setting signal to the *governor*, dependent on the desired number of RPM.

At shut-down, the fuel injection is stopped by activating the *puncture valves* in the fuel pumps, independent of the speed position of the speed setting device. The layout of the Engine Control System is shown in following Figure.

Pneumatic/Electric manoeuvring	氣動／電動操俥	Governor	調速器
Orders	俥令	Puncture valves	回油閥
Manoeuvring consoles	操俥控制台		

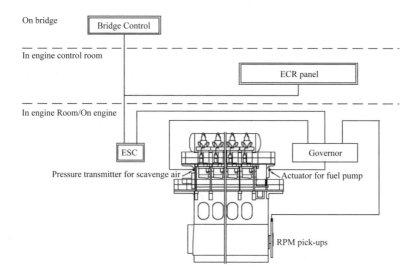

二十三、暖氣、通風及冷氣（Heating, Ventilation and Air Conditioning）

Heating, ventilation and air conditioning (HVAC) systems on commercial cargo ships are not large consumers of power, but there are several ways to improve efficiency and reduce the required power. In the case of air conditioning (AC) and heating systems, one way to reduce the power load is to provide for energy transfer between the incoming air and the exhausting air. This allows the cool air being *exhausted* from the air conditioned *accommodation* to pre-cool the incoming air, and similarly in winter months to heat the incoming air with the warm air being exhausted.

The energy transfer can be carried out by installing a simple *circu-*

lating system comprising a pump and heating/cooling coils in the main supply and *exhaust ducts*. Other systems have been used for large cruise ships that require a rotating bed that passes through one duct and then the other, but these require the ducts to be adjacent to each other, require more space and can be expensive.

Automated AC control systems can also be supplied that monitor actual demand on the system and control the system to provide a variable capacity *sufficient to* meet the need rather than operating at full capacity all of the time. Machinery space supply fans often have rather large motors, many of which are two-speed. When heat generation due to engine loads and combustion air requirements are reduced, fans should be secured or slowed down to match the actual ventilation requirements.

Exhausted	排出的氣	Comprising	包含
Accommodation	住艙	Exhaust ducts	排氣管
Circulating system	循環系統	Sufficient to	足以

二十四、甲板機械（Deck Machinery）

Mariner deck machineries are designed in various types and drive systems. The commonly used winches are the electro hydraulic driven and direct marine electric motor driven types. For both drive systems *automatic self-tension* types and remote controlled type winches are included in mariner's scope of delivery.

Different mariner deck machinery types include: anchor windlass / mooring winches, mooring winches, aft anchor winches, chain stoppers, *single point mooring* (*SPM*) chain stoppers, vertical capstans, towing winches, *tugger* winches and positioning winches. Winches with spooling devices suitable for extreme operation conditions are also available by mariner.

Developments in winches and other deck machinery continue to *keep pace with* the current trends in shipbuilding and repair worldwide. This is especially true for the so-called *high performance winches* and cranes used in a variety of traditional and new ventures. This class of machinery exhibits exceptional operating characteristics often *tailored to* a vessel or *class specific* mission.

The latest generation of *variable frequency* (VF) electric winch drive offers performance equal to or greater than many hydraulic systems, and requires less maintenance. Hydraulic valves, controls, and motors have continued to improve and still offer very good performance and value in many applications. The main problem with hydraulics is that the minute you turn them on they start wearing themselves out. Therefore leaks and even *catastrophic failure* can occur, not to mention the far higher costs associated with installing a hydraulic system.

Much has been written about the *legitimate benefits* and drawbacks of electric versus hydraulic power for deck machinery, but less has been said about the change to electric that has become the predominant customer preference in many applications.

Automatic self-tension	張力自動調整	**Tailored to**	量身訂作
Single point mooring (SPM)	單點繫泊	**Class specific**	配合船級
Tugger	拖船	**Variable frequency**	變頻
Keep pace with	跟上步調	**Catastrophic failure**	災難型故障
High performance winches	高性能吊桿	**Legitimate benefits**	該有的利益

第四節　輪機說明書（Manual for Marine Engineering）

　　讀說明書，可說是輪機員勝任輪機工作的根本。請讀者先反覆朗讀以下短文，並盡可能一面聯想在機艙裡的實務工作。

　　For a Marine Engineer, there are plenty of things to be learned from experience that can't be gained from a standard textbook. Here are some __ to help a Marine Engineer understand their ship in a better way.

　　Machinery systems differ from one ship to the next. This means the operating and maintenance procedures may differ significantly. For example, it's important for a Marine Engineer to understand *starting and stopping procedures*.

　　The answer for learning these procedures is found in the *technical manuals*. Read them and keep them nearby. The manual holds the key to all the maintenance schedules, as well as *troubleshooting tips*. Keeping good *repair records* will tell the story of your engine and help the engineer schedule *routine maintenance* and *anticipate frequent repairs*.

　　Reports on past repairs will also let the engineer know what problems have presented themselves frequently and how the engine room *behaves in specific conditions*. Different *technical specs* of the engine like bearing and *bumping clearances* in compressor areas play a key role in maintenance systems. Knowing this data will help the engineer plan out and schedule regular maintenance.

　　Anytime a major repair is done on the crank shaft through *grinding*, the size and fit of the *adjoining parts* will also be altered. Double check the repair records to make sure you buy the correct parts for the jobs. Once you understand what repairs need to be done most often, stocking the necessary parts becomes clear and will save you from getting a *major headache* at sea.

Important engine room machinery generally has *a test built in to gauge* how efficiently everything is running. It's obviously important that a Marine Engineer understands these tests and how *to perform* them.

Starting and stopping procedures	起停程序	**Bumping clearances**	震動間隙
Technical manuals	說明書	**Grinding**	研磨
Troubleshooting tips	故障診斷要領	**Adjoining parts**	毗鄰部位
Repair records	修理紀錄	**Major headache**	很頭痛、大麻煩
Routine maintenance	定期保養	**A test built in**	內設的測試儀
Anticipate frequent repairs	預測經常性修理	**To gauge**	用以量測
Behaves in specific conditions	特殊狀況下的作為	**To perform**	操作
Technical specs	技術規格		

一、柴油主機（Main Diesel Engine）

 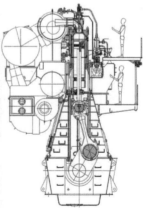

引擎型號（Engine type）以MAN B&W 主機為例，若引擎名牌上載明型號為6S70MC-C7，對照下圖，可知這部引擎有六個氣缸，超長

行程,活塞內徑70 cm,M型、凸輪軸控制、噴油、精實引擎為第7版。

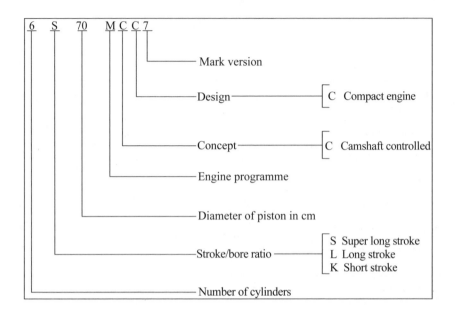

某船MAN B&W主機型號說明

　　一般而言,船上的說明書可分為使用說明書、操作說明書及保養說明書三類,分別由船上各機器的製造廠商提供。以下分別介紹,請透過反覆朗讀,了解它們各有什麼用處。

二、使用說明書(Instruction Manual)

　　The instruction manual provides the overall review of the machinery or system, within which the working principles, the performance reports and the detailed engineering drawings in association with the machinery are included. Nevertheless, most of the working principles for a variety of shipping machineries have been collected in the standard text books for students majored in Marine Engineering. The review of the instruction manual along with the on board practice will be beneficial for understanding the contents of text books. Figure below shows a typical sea water pump used for ballasting, cooling, and/or general service. Information regarding characteristics of the motor and pump is illustrated beside the draw.

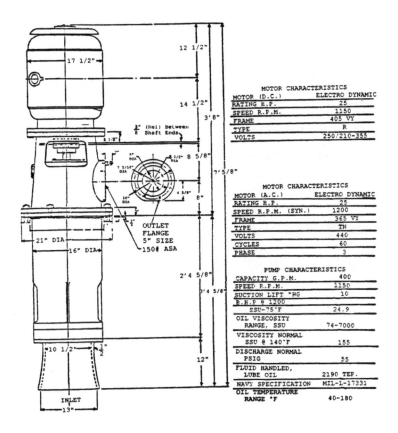

三、操作說明書（Operational Manual）

The operation manual is devised to assist the engineer to become familiar with the machinery and to utilize this machinery in its intended application. The operation manual generally provides important instruc-

輪機英文

tions as to the safe, accurate and efficient operation of the machinery. Particularly, the operation manual contains the useful information on how to identify the hazards at the earliest stage and to avoid these hazardous events. The accurate operation manners aimed at improving the reliability and the service life of the machinery are also included in the operation manual. As a result, the operation manual must be available at all times at the site of the operation by all persons working with the machinery. It is also essential to read the operation manual before beginning operation by all persons working with the machinery. Even the personnel only works with the particular machinery occasionally, the operation manual must have been read and understood before working on this machinery. All the instructions stated in the operation manual need to be followed. This applies particularly to the safety aspects.

四、保養說明書（Maintenance Manual）

In a maintenance manual, the checking and maintenance schedules which indicate the intervals of machinery components at which are deemed appropriate to inspect and to carry out overhauls, the working procedures for each major maintenance work, the usages of the special tools provided by the manufacturer for each particular maintenance work and the standard specifications for components of a machinery are included. Depending on the engine condition or on the time criteria, the additional maintenance works or the overhauls are necessary. The Normal Hours of Services, which are generally stated in a maintenance manual for determining the interval of maintenance for the machinery components, shall be used as a general guide.

Using a diesel engine as an illustrative example, the differences between the actual service conditions, the fuel quality, the conditions of lubricant oil system and the treatment of cooling water system play the decisive roles on the actual service results. Therefore the intervals between the necessary overhauling for the same machinery component vary with the actual servicing conditions.

With the after service modifications on the machinery, the revision of the instructions in the maintenance manual is necessary. In addition to the maintenance schedules stated in the maintenance manual for the major components of machinery, the periodical survey requirements of the classification society may require the additional checks or overhauls to be carried out. These additional maintenance works have to be complied with the regulations set by the associated classification societies.

The MAN B&W MC/MC-C engine combines classic virtues of commonly known, well-proven technology continuously upgraded and up-rated to suit the requirements to modern prime movers. The engine concept is based on a mechanical camshaft system for activation of the fuel injection and the exhaust valves. The engine is provided with a pneumatic/electric manoeuvring system and the engine speed is controlled by an electronic/hydraulic type governor.

- Each cylinder is equipped with its own fuel injection pump, which consists of a simple plunger activated by the fuel cam directly.

- Fuel economy at part load is optimized by means of the Variable Injection Timing (VIT) incorporated in the fuel pumps.

- The cam controlled exhaust valve is opened hydraulically and closed by means of an air spring.

- Lubrication is either by means of a uni-lube oil system serving crankshaft, chain drive, piston cooling and camshaft or a combination of a main lubricating oil system and a separate camshaft lube oil system.

- The starting valves are opened pneumatically by control air from the starting air distributor(s) and closed by a spring.

五、柴油引擎保養說明書（Maintenance Manual of a Diesel Engine）

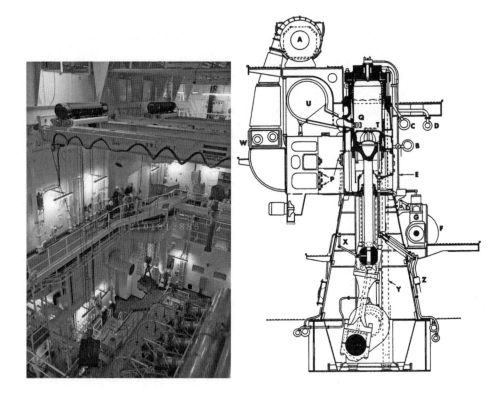

For this particular maintenance manual, the maintenance procedures required after normal hours of service are divided into three categories, namely the Condition checking procedure, the Condition-based overhauling procedures and the Time-based overhauling procedures with the specific abbreviations quoted for these three categories. The checking and maintenance schedules for this diesel engine are generally provided as the essential table in a maintenance manual. In what follows, the maintenance schedules as well as the work procedures for the major maintenance works are re-edited from.

六、保養說明書實例：油水分離器（Maintaining the OWS）

The OWS requires regular maintenance, including the following cleaning and inspection procedures, to operate most efficiently and effectively. Never enter the OWS, the riser, the manway extension or any other enclosed space without proper training and OSHA-approved equipment. See OSHA guidelines 29 CFR, Part 1910 "Permit Required Confined Spaces." Failure to follow this warning could result in death or serious injury.

1. Ventilate all enclosed spaces according to methods described in applicable regulations and codes before entering an OWS to avoid asphyxiation or ignition of vapors or liquid oil, which are flammable. Failure to properly ventilate could result in death or serious injury. OWS interior surfaces are slippery. A slip or fall could result in death or serious injury.

2. Perform maintenance at least once a year.

3. Under the following conditions, maintenance is required more frequently:

- if the OWS bottom sludge accumulation is more than 12 inches deep;
- when the effluent water exceeds the effluent quality level mandated by applicable federal, state and local codes and regulations;
- after a major oil spill has occurred.

CLEANING THE OWS

Begin maintenance by cleaning the OWS, using the following procedure:

1. Remove all liquid from the OWS before entering the OWS. Properly dispose of oil removed from the OWS as required by federal, state and local laws, codes and regulations.

2. Close inlet and outlet piping valves if present or plug the piping before entering the OWS. Failure to close inlet and outlet piping valves or plug the piping before entering the OWS could result in death or serious injury.

3. Remove the coalescer for cleaning. Do not stand on the coalescer support grating. This grating is slippery and a slip or fall could result in death or serious injury.

4. Suction or shovel out sludge and debris from the OWS. Do not use picks, axes, hammers or other heavy tools or objects when breaking apart sludge in the OWS. Such tools may damage the OWS. When using a shovel to remove sludge, do not strike the OWS. Striking the OWS may damage it.

5. Loosen any caked oily solids in the OWS by spraying with a standard garden hose (with or without a spray nozzle) at a pressure between 40 and 70 psig.

6. Use hot water for best results. Do not use detergent or soap. Do not use soaps or detergents when cleaning the coalescers. Soaps or detergents may damage the coalescers and/or reduce the efficiency of the OWS.

7. Aim the flow of water at the OWS walls — top, sides and bottom.

8. Shovel out the slurry, being careful not to damage the OWS.

9. Check the oil/water sensor (if installed) for movement.

10. Remove and clean the sensor if the floats do not easily slide on the stem or if there is sludge on the floats.

11. Visually inspect the OWS interior (walls, components and inlet piping) for damage. If you observe any damage, contact the Xerxes manufacturing facility from which the OWS was shipped. (See telephone numbers on back of OWS Manual.)

12. Install the cleaned coalescer packs, support grating and retaining

pieces by reversing the steps.

13. If the coalescer packs are not properly installed, the OWS will not work properly or efficiently. Check to see that the coalescer packs, support grating and retaining pieces are reinstalled properly. Improper installation may result in damage to the OWS and/or reduce its efficiency.

14. Attach the manway lid.

15. Check to see that the gaskets are not damaged.

16. Replace gaskets as necessary.

17. Charge the OWS by filling it half-full with clean water.

18. Restart the OWS.

第五節　簡短溝通（Short Communication）

　　在輪機工作當中，人員之間的溝通，往往是決定能否順利共同完成任務的關鍵。只是在大多實際工作場合當中，為能有效溝通，工作人員通常採取的是極簡短的溝通，其中包括手勢和圖像、符號等交互運用的方式。

一、緊急狀況（Emergency Situation）

　　船上可能遇到的緊急狀況如下，試著理解它們究竟是些什麼狀況。

Enclosed space	封閉艙間	Cargo holds	貨艙
Man overboard	人員落水	Collision	撞船
Grounding	觸礁	Oil spill	溢油

Accident in an enclosed space

Fire in the cargo holds

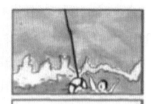

Man overboard

Fire in the galley

Collision

Grounding

Oil spill

Electrical fire

二、標誌與符號（Symbols and Signs）

　　船上可能出現的標誌與符號如下，試著理解它們代表什麼意思，以及看到它們時應該注意什麼事情。

連連看：

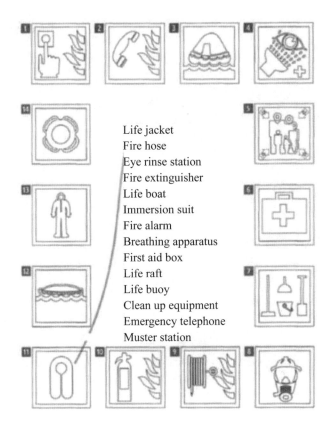

Life jacket
Fire hose
Eye rinse station
Fire extinguisher
Life boat
Immersion suit
Fire alarm
Breathing apparatus
First aid box
Life raft
Life buoy
Clean up equipment
Emergency telephone
Muster station

Eye rinse station	眼睛清洗站	Immersion suit	浸水衣
Breathing apparatus (BA)	呼吸器	Muster station	緊急集合站

三、容器的類型（Types of Containers）

船上以各類型容器來盛裝不同的東西，試著理解它們的用途。

連連看：

Type of container 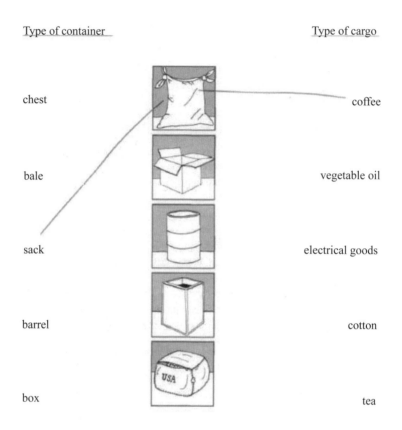 Type of cargo

chest   coffee

bale   vegetable oil

sack   electrical goods

barrel   cotton

box   tea

以下舉出在機艙的管輪和駕駛台的船副，必須採取適當溝通的十個最重要的情況。

（一）機艙機器失常

A machinery in the ship's engine room is bound to face problem when at sea. In case of breakdown of any machinery, the Duty Engineer must inform the bridge officer immediately without any delay. If problem occurs in the main engine, power generator or any associated machinery which can affect the voyage of the ship, the engineer must take all necessary steps and inform the bridge at the earliest.

（二）船上起火

With implementation of advanced safety and automation systems, detection of fire on board ships has become quite efficient. In case of fire on the ship, the indication of affected location is displayed in the fire station. In such condition, it is important that Duty Engineer call the duty officer to inform about the specific location of fire even after the fire alarm has been sounded. The same rule also applies to the duty officer, who must inform the bridge on how big is the fire and its condition after ringing the fire alarm. However, only informing is not important, it is necessary that all required steps are taken by the ship's crew to stop the fire and inform other department regarding the same.

（三）起霧、交通擁擠、穿越大橋等狀況

Today, most of the ships have UMS engine room and the engine is controlled from the bridge. If any situation arises wherein the engine is to be slowed down and manned, the bridge officer must inform the Duty Engineer well in advance. These situation may include: Fog or weather warning, Canal Crossing, High Traffic Areas, Under-Bridge Crossing etc.

（四）煙囪冒出濃煙、火花

If the ship's funnel is discharging abnormal black/ white smoke or there are sparks rising from the funnel, the deck officer on the bridge must inform the same to the engine room immediately as it may lead to uptake fire if ignored.

（五）船內駁油

Any engine room internal oil transfer procedure must be pre-informed to the bridge officer as the transfer of oil from one tank to another may affect the current list/ trim of the ship. Also, an informed deck officer will keep a good overboard watch and revert back to the engine room immediately in case of oil leakage or spill.

（六）泵水

Ballast pumps are high capacity pumps which are used to correct the list, trim or draught of the ship. They are also used in ports for cargo loading/ discharging. In order to save fuel, normally one generator is run at higher load when the ship is at port. Hence deck officer must inform the engine department before starting any pumps including ballast and fire pump as there might be a requirement to start one more generators to accommodate the power requirement.

（七）操作甲板機械

Before starting any deck machinery including bow thrusters and winches, the deck officer must inform the engine department so that engineers can check and ensure that the machinery is ready to start and the generator has enough accommodating power available. Also, in case of bow thruster (BT), hydraulic pumps and fans are to be started sequentially before the main operation, which the ship engineer will perform if informed well in advance.

（八）操作油水分離器

Nowadays, Oily Water Separator is an important ship machinery checked by all PSCs on every visit. It is important for Marine Engineers to inform the bridge and take position of the ship while starting and stopping the Oily Water Separator. Also, bridge officers are required to take a note of the same in the bridge log book. An overside check is also required by the bridge officer for any oil sheen in water once the OWS operation has started. Oil pollution from ship is a serious crime which includes huge fines and even imprisonment. OWS operation therefore requires clear and sound communication between officers from both the departments.

（九）機艙有人或無人當值

Engine officer on duty of a UMS ship must inform the bridge before turning on the Unmanned mode and leaving the engine room. Engineer should inform about his visit and manned/unmanned situation every time he/she visits the engine room and switch on or switch off the dead man's alarm. This will help in informing the bridge officer of an engineer's presence in the machinery space. Also, in case of any mishap in the engine room or "no reply" of the dead man's alarm, the deck officer can assist and take immediate action.

（十）領港、PSC上船

It is the duty of the bridge officer to inform the engine room about the pilot boarding time or whenever any outside authority is about to visit the ship. This will give time to engine room staff to be ready for important situations and prevent any kind of ship delay.

第六節　輪機新知

輪機技術日新月異。尤其隨著國際間「環境優先」共識的形成與持續推進，對於船運業的要求事項也快速增加，其中大多與輪機關係密切。接觸新知、持續進修也就成了當今輪機員必須做到的。本章接下來要利用以下短文，舉例介紹許多輪機員可能在接下來的數年當中，容易接觸到，且必須清楚了解的一些信息。請反覆朗誦，並在讀的過程中想想其中的意思。

一、引擎減出力和降低轉速（Reducing Engine Output and RPM）

An engine's SFOC is affected by various factors that can improve its efficiency and that of the propulsion system. The *thermodynamic efficiency* of the engine is affected by the ratio of *maximum firing pressure* to *mean effective pressure*, with a higher ratio resulting in lower SFOC.

Selecting an engine with a higher maximum MCR than is required for the vessel and de-rating it to a lower MCR power that meets the *design performance* of a ship will result in the *de-rated* MCR power being developed at a lower mean effective pressure.

That allows *optimization* of the *combustion process* rather than maximization of the power output thereby improving fuel efficiency. De-rating an existing engine would result in slowing down the maximum speed of the ship.

Costs for a de-rated engine installation are *indeterminate* as they depend on the effect of a larger engine, on the engine room arrangement and the ship design. In addition, the cost may depend on the *shipyard market situation* at the time of *bidding*. Shipyards may offer lower fuel consumption design at no extra cost to obtain orders when fuel prices are high.

Energy Efficiency Design Index (EEDI) impact of a de-rated engine should be *favourable* since the fuel consumption goes down for the same power and speed used for the vessel inputs into the EEDI equation. Note that *uprating* a de-rated engine (back to its design MCR to increase speed) may only be possible if the related engine auxiliary systems (including shafting) are originally designed and installed to match the larger rating. The EEDI would also have to be within *baseline limits* with the larger rating.

Thermodynamic efficiency	熱力效率	Indeterminate	不定
Maximum firing pressure	最高燃燒壓力	Shipyard market situation	造船市場情況
Mean effective pressure	平均有效壓力	Bidding	招標
Design performance	設計性能	Energy efficiency design index	能源效率設計指標
De-rated	減功率	Favourable	有利的
Optimization	最佳化	Uprating	提高出力
Combustion process	燃燒過程	Baseline limits	基線範圍

二、燃料考量（Fuel Considerations）

When the engine is stopped, the *circulating pump* will continue to circulate heated HFO through the fuel oil system on the engine, thereby keeping the fuel pumps heated and the fuel valves *deaerated*. This automatic circulation of preheated fuel during engine stand still is the background for our recommendation: constant operation on heavy fuel.

If this recommendation was not followed, there would be a latent risk of diesel oil and heavy fuels of marginal quality forming *incompatible blends* during fuel change over or when operating in areas with restrictions on sulphur content in fuel oil due to exhaust gas emission control. In special circumstances a changeover to diesel oil may become necessary – and this can be performed at any time, even when the engine is not running.

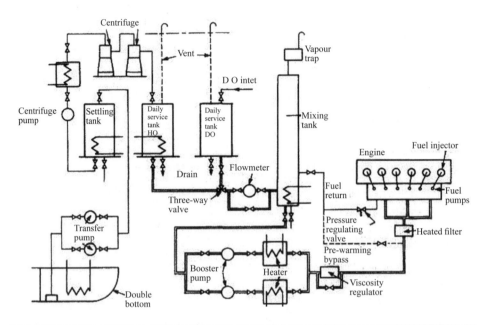

Circulating pump	循環泵	Deaerated	去除空氣
Incompatible blends	不相容混合物		

三、燃油乳化系統（Fuel Oil Emulsification System）

The emulsification of water into the fuel oil reduces the NO_x emission with about 1% per 1% water added to the fuel up to about 20% without modification of the engine fuel injection equipment. A *water in fuel emulsion* (WIF) mixed for this purpose and based on HFO is stable for a long time, whereas a WIF based on *marine diesel oil* (MDO) is only stable for a short period of time unless an emulsifying agent is applied.

As both the MAN B&W two-stroke main engine and the MAN Diesel GenSets are designed to run on emulsified HFO, it can be used for a common system. It is supposed below, that both the main engine and

GenSets are running on the same fuel, either HFO or a homogenized HFO-based WIF. Special arrangements are available on request for a more sophisticated system in which the GenSets can run with or without a homogenized HFO based WIF, if the main engine is running on that. Please note that the *fuel pump injection capacity* shall be confirmed for the main engine as well as the GenSets for the selected percentage of water in the WIF.

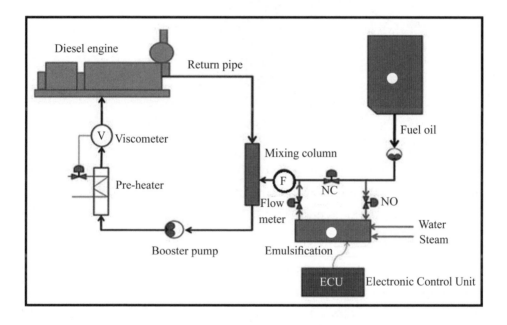

Water in fuel emulsion	燃油水乳化	Marine diesel oil	海運（船用）柴油
Fuel pump injection capacity	燃油泵噴射量		

四、共軌系統（Common Rail System）

As shown in above figure, although common-rail fuel injection is not a new idea, it has only become truly practical in recent years

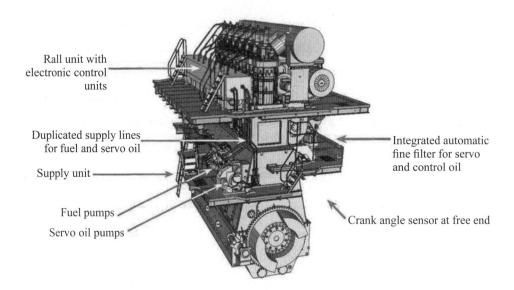

Rall unit with electronic control units

Duplicated supply lines for fuel and servo oil

Supply unit

Fuel pumps

Servo oil pumps

Integrated automatic fine filter for servo and control oil

Crank angle sensor at free end

through the use of *fully-integrated electronic control* based on high-performance computers which allow the best use to be made of the *flexibility* possible with common-rail injection.

The traditional camshaft has the considerable limitation of fixed timing given mechanically by the cams. Although Sulzer low-speed engines have long had the benefits of double valve-controlled fuel injection pumps with *variable injection timing* (VIT), and a degree of *variable exhaust valve timing* being achieved hydraulically in the variable exhaust valve closing (VEC) system, the variation in timing so obtained has been very limited.

The common-rail concept was adopted also because it has the advantage that the functions of pumping and injection control are separated. This allows a *straightforward* approach to the mechanical and hydraulic aspects of the design, with a steady generation of fuel oil supply at the desired pressure ready for injection.

The combined flexibilities of common rail and electronic control thus provide improved low-speed operation, engine *acceleration*, balance between cylinders, load control, and longer times between *overhauls*. They also ensure better combustion at all operating speeds and loads, giving benefits in lower fuel consumption, lower *exhaust emissions* in terms of both smokeless operation at all operating speeds and less NO_x emissions, and also a cleaner engine internally with less *deposit* of combustion *residues*. Engine *diagnostics* are built into the system, improving engine *monitoring*, *reliability* and *availability*.

Fully-integrated electronic control	完整電子控制	Exhaust emissions	廢氣排放
Flexibility	彈性	Deposit	沉積物
Variable injection timing	變動噴燃正時	Residues	殘渣
Variable exhaust valve timing	變動排氣閥正時	Diagnostics	診斷
Straightforward	單純的	Monitoring	監測
Acceleration	加速	Reliability	可靠性
Overhauls	吊缸	Availability	可用性

五、高效率過給氣機和傳統過給氣機的油耗率（SFOC for High Efficiency/Conventional Turbocharger）

All engine types are as standard fitted with high efficiency turbochargers but can *alternatively* use conventional turbochargers. The high efficiency turbocharger is applied to the engine in the basic design with the view to obtaining the lowest possible SFOC values. With a conventional turbocharger the amount of air required for combustion purposes can, however, be adjusted to provide a higher exhaust gas temperature, if this is needed for the *exhaust gas boiler*.

The matching of the engine and the turbocharging system is then modified, thus increasing the exhaust gas temperature by 20°C.This *modification* will lead to a 7-8% reduction in the exhaust gas amount, and involve an *SFOC penalty* of 2 g/kWh, see curve below.

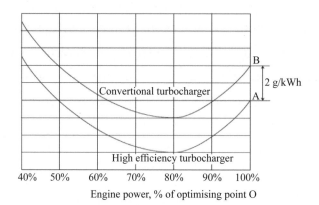

Engine power, % of optimising point O

Alternatively	或者亦可	**Modification**	調整
Exhaust gas boiler	排氣鍋爐	**SFOC penalty**	SFOC折損

六、大氣排放防制（Atmospheric Emission Control）──氮氧化物排放限制與減量方法（NO_x Emission Limits and NO_x Reduction Methods）

The NO_x content in the exhaust gas can be reduced with primary and/or secondary *reduction* methods. The *primary methods* affect the *combustion process* directly by reducing the maximum combustion temperature, whereas the *secondary methods* are means of reducing the emission level without changing the engine performance, using *external equipment*.

（一）減少30%以下的氮氧化物（0～30% NOx Reduction）

The MC and MC-C engines are as standard delivered to comply with International Maritime Organization (IMO) NOx emission limitations. Regardless of the emission limit specified, the engines are matched for *best economy in service*.

（二）減少30%至50% 氮氧化物（30～50% NOx Reduction）

Water *emulsification* of the HFO is a well proven primary method. The type of *homogenizer* is either *ultrasonic* or mechanical, using water from the freshwater generator and the water *mist catcher*. The pressure of the homogenized fuel has to be increased to prevent the formation of steam and *cavitation*. It may be necessary to modify some of the engine components such as the fuel oil *pressure booster*, fuel injection valves and the engine control system.

（三）減少氮氧化物達95%至98%（ Up to 95～98% NOx Reduction）

When operating at full load, this reduction can be achieved by means of secondary methods, such as the *SCR* (Selective Catalytic Reduction), which involves an after treatment of the exhaust gas. At lower load a 80-90% NOx reduction can be obtained.

Reduction	還原	Homogenizer	均質機
Primary methods	初級方法	Ultrasonic	超音波
Combustion process	燃燒過程	Mist catcher	集霧器
Secondary methods	次級方法	Cavitation	空蝕
External equipment	外加設備	Pressure booster	增壓機
Best economy in service	運轉最佳經濟性	SCR	選擇性催化還原
Emulsification	乳化		

七、輔助功率輸出裝置（Power Take Off）

With a generator coupled to a *Power Take Off* (PTO) from the main engine, electrical power can be produced based on the main engine's low SFOC and the use of heavy fuel oil. Several standardized PTO systems are available:

- PTO/RCF (Power Take Off/*Renk Constant Frequency*): Generator giving constant frequency, based on mechanical-hydraulical speed control.

- PTO/CFE (Power Take Off/*Constant Frequency Electrical*):Generator giving constant frequency, based on electrical frequency control.

The DMG/CFE (*Direct Mounted Generator*/Constant Frequency Electrical) and the SMG/CFE (*Shaft Mounted Generator*/Constant Frequency Electrical) are special designs within the PTO/CFE group in which the generator is coupled directly to the main engine crankshaft and the *intermediate shaft*, respectively, without a gear. The electrical output of the generator is controlled by electrical frequency control. Within each PTO system, several designs are available, depending on the positioning of the gear.

Alternative types and layouts of shaft generators		Design	Seating	Total efficiency (%)
PTO/RGF	1a ⊷ 1b ▭ 0000 ⊙	BW I/RCF	On engine (vertical generator)	88-91
	2a ⊷ 2b 0000 ⊙	BW II/RCF	On tank top	88-91
	3a ⊷ 3b 0000 ⊙	BW III/RCF	On engine	88-91
	4a ⊷ 4b 0000	BW IV/RCF	On tank top	88-91
PTO/CFE	5a ⊷ 5b 0000 ⊙	DMG/CFE	On engine	84-88
	6a ⊷ 6b ⊙ 0000	SMG/CFE	On tank top	84-88

Power take off	分力器	Renk constant frequency	Renk定頻器
Constant frequency electrical	定頻電動	Shaft mounted generator	軸發電機
Direct mounted generator	直接裝設發電機	Intermediate shaft	中間軸

八、裝置型號（Model）

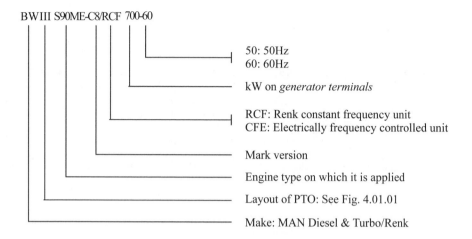

BWIII S90ME-C8/RCF 700-60

- 50: 50Hz
- 60: 60Hz
- kW on *generator terminals*
- RCF: Renk constant frequency unit
- CFE: Electrically frequency controlled unit
- Mark version
- Engine type on which it is applied
- Layout of PTO: See Fig. 4.01.01
- Make: MAN Diesel & Turbo/Renk

Generator terminals	發電機終端		

九、新一代柴油引擎（New Generation of Diesel Engines）

Camshaft-controlled diesel engines have been the state of the art ever since the birth of *reciprocating machinery* and have been refined and developed ever since. However, a mechanical cam is fixed once made and, in spite of various mechanical and hydraulic add-on devices like VIT, etc., timing control possibilities are limited with mechanical cams. Not least fuel injection pressure control and variation over the load range have limitations with a cam-controlled engine. Therefore, the main purpose of changing to electronic control is to ensure fuel injection timing and rate, as well as the exhaust valve timing and operation, exactly when and as desired. Especially with respect to the fuel injection rate, the control system has been so designed that it is possible to maintain a rather high injection pressure also at low load, without the limitation from the camshaft-controlled engine, where this would result in too high pressure at high load. Both the 'cam angle, inclination and length' are electronically variable.

In addition, the ME engine of MAN B&W features electronic control of the cylinder lube oil. With the Alpha Lubrication system, about 0.3 g/bhp-h cylinder oil can be saved, compared with engines with mechanical lubricators. The electronic control of the engine fuel injection and exhaust valves improves low-load operation, engine acceleration, and give better engine balance and load control, leading to longer *times between overhauls*, also by implementation of enhanced diagnostics systems. It will give lower fuel consumption, lower cylinder oil consumption and, not least, better emission characteristics, particularly with regard to visible smoke and NO_x.

The ME engine features fully integrated control of all functions like the governor, start and reversing, fuel, exhaust and starting valves, as well as cylinder oil feeding. The following parts are omitted:

- Chain drive
- Chain wheel frame
- Chain box on frame box
- Camshaft with cams
- Roller guides for fuel pumps and exhaust valves
- Fuel injection pumps
- Exhaust valve actuators
- Starting air distributor
- Governor
- Regulating shaft
- Mechanical cylinder lubricator
- Local control stand

| Reciprocating machinery | 往復機械 | Time between overhauls | 吊缸間隔 |

十、雙燃料引擎（ME-GI Dual Fuel MAN B&W Engines）

Market research indicates that, in future, gas applications may be installed not only on LNG carriers, but also on LPG, RoRo, and container vessels, i.e.in principle all types of vessels.

In principle, there are three different solutions for combining the gas supply system with the MAN B&W two-stroke ME-GI. The three solutions are listed below:

- use of the high-pressure BOG compressor.
- use of reliquefaction plant and high pressure LNG pumps.
- use of reliquefaction plant and high pressure BOG compressor.

The decision to invest in *dual-fuelled vessels* will be based primarily on the owners' expectations for the future development in gas and fuel oil prices, safety regulations and emission control regulations.

Results from studies show that dual fuel engines can be more than just *economically sound* – dual fuel engines are also safe, reliable and *environmentally desirable*, as a result of the experience obtained through many years from two-stroke diesel engines for the marine market for single as well as *double-propeller vessels* in all types of commercial application.

Beyond the whole question of price, safety, reliability and availability are the main parameters when shipowners and operators select *prime movers* for vessels in their fleets.

More specifically for LNG carriers, the type of gas supply system seems to depend on the type of application of the LNG carrier, e.g. operation as *carrier train* between two destinations, or spot market trading.

The technology for a gas driven two stroke ME-GI engine is available – and ready to install. However, different applications can call for different gas supply systems, and recent projects have shown that operators and shipowners demand an alternative to the gas compressor solutions.

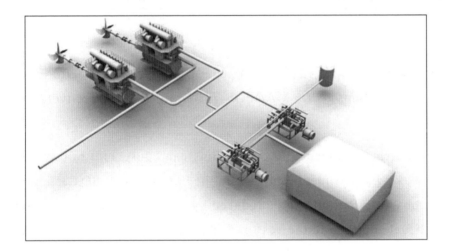

The GI system also includes:

- Control and safety system, comprising a *hydrocarbon analyzer* for checking the hydrocarbon content of the air in the double-wall gas pipes...
- The GI control and safety system is designed to "fail to safe condition". All failures detected during gas fuel running, including failures of the control system itself, will result in a gas fuel Stop/Shutdown, and a change-over to HFO fuel operation.
- Blow-out and *gas freeing purging* of the high-pressure gas pipes and of the complete gas supply system follows.

The change-over to fuel oil mode is always done without any power loss on the engine. The high-pressure gas from the gas supply flows through the main pipe via narrow and flexible branch pipes to each cylinder's gas valve block system and accumulator.

Dual fuel vessel	雙燃料船	Economically sound	合乎經濟的
Environmental desirable	符合環保的	Double-propeller vessel	雙螺槳船
Prime mover	原動機	Carrier train	運輸系列
Hydrocarbon analyzer	碳氫化合物分析儀	Gas freeing purging	排氣清除

十一、船舶大氣排放相關法規（Legal Basis for Atmospheric Emission from Ships）──MARPOL 73/78 Annex VI Directive 2005/33/EC

Problem Statement: SOx emissions can cause acid rain in coastal areas having a detrimental impact on the environment. SOx as a product of combusting fuel oil can be reduced by decreasing the sulphur content in the fuel supplied to the vessel. Reduction of SOx can be achieved by the after treatment of the exhaust gases from engines and boilers via cleaning. The sulphur content of fuel influences the emissions of particulates. Less sulphur means less *particulate matter* (PM).

Particulates matter	微粒、粒狀物		

十二、港口國管制（Port State Control）

It is known that the responsibility for ensuring that ships comply with the provisions of the *relevant instruments* rests upon the owners, masters and the *flag States*. Some flag States fail to fulfill their commitments contained in agreed international legal instruments and subsequently some ships are sailing in an unsafe condition, threatening the lives as well as the marine environment. Port State Control (PSC) is a system of *harmonized inspection procedures* designed to target *sub-standards ships* with the main objective being their eventual elimination. Co-operation between flag State and Port State Having recognized that the main responsibility lies with the flag State on the one hand and the inability for a variety of reasons of some of flag States to meet, entirely, their obligations under the conventions resulting in the existence of substandard ships it is imperative to develop close co-operation between flag States and port States.

It is a fact that the most important largest Registries have become so due to the attraction of ships whose *beneficial ownership* belongs to traditional maritime countries which again, for a variety of reasons have chosen a particular port of regulation as oppose to others. It is in the best interest of all to develop effective Flag State/Port State *interfaces* for the sake of safe shipping.

Relevant instrument	相關儀器	**Flag state**	船旗國
Harmonized inspection procedure	經協調檢驗程序	**Substandard ship**	次標準船
Beneficial ownership	受益所有權	**Interfaces**	介面

十三、散裝輪推進的趨勢（Trend of Bulker Propulsion）

The demand for *raw materials* like coal, steel, copper, etc., has increased considerably since the turn of the *millennium*, especially in consequence of globalization and the great demand for raw materials in China.

The *optimum propeller speed* is changing as well, steadily becoming lower, because the larger the propeller diameter that can be used for a ship, the actual propeller power and *pertaining speed requirement* will be correspondingly lower, and the lower the propulsion power demand per ton bulk transported.

These factors have an influence on which main engine type should be selected/installed as the prime mover, and also on the size of the bulk carrier to be built. Recent development steps have made it possible to offer solutions which will enable significantly lower transportation costs for bulk carriers.

One of the goals in the marine industry today is to reduce the impact of CO_2 emissions from ships and, therefore, to reduce the fuel consumption for the propulsion of ships to the widest possible extent at any load. This also means that the inherent design CO_2 index of a new ship, the so call *Energy Efficiency Design Index* (EEDI), will be reduced. Based on an average reference CO_2 emission from existing bulk carriers, the CO_2 emission from new bulk carriers in gram per *dead weight* (DWT) per nautical mile must be equal to or lower than the *reference emission figures* valid for the specific bulk carrier.

This drive results in operation at lower than normal service ship speeds compared to earlier. The propulsion power utilization is therefore reduced. However, it still seems to be unchanged. A more technically advanced development drive is to optimize the *aftbody* and *hull lines* of the ship – including *bulbous bow*, also considering operation *in ballast condition*. This makes it possible to install propellers with a larger diameter and, thereby, obtaining higher *propeller efficiency*, but at a reduced speed, i.e. using less power for the same ship speed.

As the two-stroke main engine is directly coupled with the propeller, the introduction of the latest MAN B&W ultra long stroke G engine types meets this trend of installing large propellers in the bulk carriers which may reduce the ship's fuel consumption.

Raw materials	原物料	Millennium	千禧年
Optimum propeller speed	最佳螺槳轉速	Pertaining speed requirement	相配速需求
Energy efficiency design index	能源效率設計指標	Dead weight	載重噸
Reference emission figure	參考排放數值	Aftbody	船體艉部
Hull line	船身線	Bulbous bow	球型艏
In ballasting condition	在壓載狀態下	Propeller efficiency	螺槳效率

近幾年來，美國海岸巡防署（US Coast Guard, USCG）公布了一系列位於其水域之船舶所必須遵循的法規，以下分成：空氣污染、油污染、污水與灰水、有害廢棄物、垃圾、壓艙水與錨鍊水、海洋生物保護等議題，舉例介紹。

十四、遵循法規之程序（Procedures for Compliance with Regulations）── Air Emissions

a. All engines shall be properly maintained and prudent start up and warm up procedures shall be *observed*. Since opacity is generally a concern when starting a cold engine and when going from a no- or low-load condition to a load condition, vessels shall adhere to maintenance schedules and plan events such as departures to include proper warm up procedures.

b. In port, vessels shall minimize operation of boilers and diesel engines by using shore-provided *hotel services* whenever operational requirements permit. *Blowing of boiler tubes* shall be limited in port to the minimum necessary.

c. Incinerators may be used per paragraph 7.B.5 of this Manual. d. Personnel shall use only authorized solvents, paints, fuels, lubricants and chemicals. The Coatings and Color Manual, M10360.3 (series) and Naval Engineering Manual, M9000.6 (series) provide guidance on authorized and unauthorized materials on vessels. The Navy standard for chemical cleaning products and *dispensing systems* authorized for use aboard surface (non-submarine) vessels (NAVSEA S6480-A4 CAT-010) has been adopted for use on Coast Guard vessels.

Observed	遵循	Hotel services	靠泊服務
Blowing of boiler tubes	爐管吹放	Dispensing system	配發系統

十五、艙底水、油及含油廢料（Bilges, Oil and Oily Waste）

a. On vessels equipped with oily water separators (OWSs) and *oil content monitors* (OCMs), OWS discharges shall be limited to those that meet the conditions: no effluent standard, including oil content, shall be achieved through dilution.

b. Equipment casualties that either threaten or result in a discharge of oily water shall be reported through the SFLC Product Line prescribed casualty reporting system. The initial report shall note the potential for discharge. All subsequent reports shall report the frequency and approximate amount of actual discharges. Chapter 9 outlines all spill-reporting requirements.

c. On vessels without an operating OWS but with an *oily waste holding tank* (OWHT), all oily water shall, to the maximum extent possible, without endangering the vessel, be directed to the OWHT for shore disposal. Equipment casualties that either threaten or result in a discharge of oily water shall be reported through the SFLC Product

Line prescribed casualty reporting system. The initial report shall note the potential for discharge. All subsequent reports shall report the frequency and approximate amount of actual discharges.

d. On vessels with neither an operating OWS nor OWHT, all oily water shall be retained for *shore disposal* to the maximum extent possible without endangering the vessel. Unpowered vessels and vessels using only outboard engines often have open-hull design and have no machinery space bilges. As such, those vessels may discharge *bilgewater / deck runoff* so long as no *visible sheen* is present. Except in an emergency, if a sheen exists, the bilgewater /deck runoff shall be retained for proper shore side disposal.

Oil content monitors	油含量監測器	Oily waste holding tank	油性廢棄物暫存櫃
Shore disposal	岸上處置	**Bilge water**	艙底水
Deck runoff	甲板逕流	**Visible sheen**	可目視油膜

十六、港內OWS之操作（Operation of OWS in Port）

Operation of the OWS in port is prohibited. Vessels shall maximize *segregation* of oily waste derived from used oils, OWS separated oils and contaminated fuel oil unless in an emergency circumstance or if the vessel is fitted with an incinerator or boiler capable of burning waste oil. *Shoreside disposal* of oily waste derived from used oils, OWS separated oils and contaminated fuel oil is the only disposal method for oily waste/used oil. Operation of the OWS shall only be conducted while underway and greater than 12 nm from shore and outside of *Special Areas*. Discharged effluent may not exceed 15 ppm (parts per million) in accordance with *MARPOL Annex I*, Regulation 15 on control of discharge of oil. Any effluent exceeding 15 ppm must be retained onboard. Operation of the OWS is strictly prohibited in MARPOL Annex I "Special Areas".

Segregation	隔離	Shoreside disposal	岸際處置
Special Areas	特別海域	MARPOL Annex I	MARPOL公約附則壹

十七、美國海岸巡防署（United States Coast Guard, USCG）對溢出事件相關要求——污水與灰水（或稱中水）（Sewage and Graywatter）

To ensure compliance with *Federal regulations* regarding sewage and graywater:

a. Vessels shall be equipped with *marine sanitation devices* (MSDs) designed to prevent the discharge of untreated or *inadequately treated sewage*, or any waste derived from sewage, within the territorial seas of the United States.

b. MSD installations shall include the capability for pumping collected sewage and graywater to appropriate shoreside *reception facilities*. Vessels shall be fitted with *cam-lock* sewage discharge connections in 4-inch, 2-1/2-inch, or 1-1/2-inch sizes, depending on the size of the vessel. Such fittings shall allow *quick connect/disconnect* with shoreside offloading hoses. Boats that have *portable* or removable MSDs are *exempted* from this requirement.

c. Although the US is not a party to MARPOL Annex IV, as a matter of policy, vessels visiting foreign ports shall be equipped with *adapters* to accommodate hoses having international-standard flanges specified by the International Maritime Organization in Annex IV, Regulation 11 of the International Convention on the Prevention of Pollution from Ships (MARPOL). Table 3-2 provides specifications for such adapters.

Federal regulations	聯邦法規	Quick connect/Disconnect	快接／快脫
Marine sanitation devices	船舶衛生設備	Portable	攜帶式
Inadequately treated sewage	未妥善處理之污水	Exempted	免除
Reception facilities	收受設施	Adapters	接頭
Cam-lock	凸輪鎖		

十八、舊潤滑油（Used Oil）

a. Maximum use shall be made of available port facilities for disposal of all waste/used oil products prior to departing and upon entering port. Facilities include *pier-side collection tanks*, tank trucks, and contaminated fuel barges.

b. *Synthetic lube oils* and hydraulic oils shall be collected separately from other waste/used oils. If a vessel is *configured to* collect used synthetic oils, personnel shall use 5 or 55-gallon steel containers, properly labeled per the Hazardous Waste Management Manual, COMDTINST M16478.1 (series) for eventual shore recycling.

c. Containers (such as *drums*, *cans*, etc.) in which oil products were originally packaged shall be reused and properly labeled per the Hazardous Waste Management Manual, COMDTINST M16478.1 (series) for storage and transfer to shore.

Pier-side collection tanks	碼頭收集櫃	Synthetic lube oils	合成潤滑油
Configured to	設定	Drums	桶，例如2,000公升
Cans	罐		

十九、有害物質與有害廢棄物管理（Hazardous Materiala and Hazardous Waste Management）——Ship-to-shore Transfer

a. Used or excess hazardous material shall be transferred to a shore activity for determination of disposition.

b. Prior to transfer ashore, hazardous material shall be identified to the receiving shore facilities per the host facility's guidance and specific requirements in accordance with established host/tenant agreements. Failure to abide by requirements may delay or even prevent offload ashore in a timely manner.

c. When visiting *non-Coast Guard ports* and foreign ports, used hazardous material shall be offloaded only when necessary and feasible. The LOGREQ shall identify the type(s) and amount of used hazardous material to be offloaded.

d. Prior to entering a shipyard for a maintenance availability:

  (1) To the maximum extent feasible, used/excess hazardous material shall be offloaded in homeport or other Coast Guard facility.

  (2) The ship hazardous material coordinator shall contact the *Ship Superintendent* or *Port Engineer*. The hazardous material coordinator shall provide a list of the types and amounts of hazardous waste anticipated by ship's force during the availability and be granted the authority and resources to ensure vessel compliance with hazardous material and waste management procedures and site specific management practices established by the Ship Superintendent or Port Engineer.

  (3) Ensure the *contractor* is aware that any hazardous waste they generate during the availability is their responsibility to handle and dispose of properly.

e. For work performed at Coast Guard facilities by Coast Guard personnel, the facility Commanding Officer or Officer in Charge shall *promulgate* instructions to ensure compliance with this Manua

Non-Coast Guard ports	非美國海岸防衛隊管轄港	Ship Superintendent	船塢經理
Port Engineer	駐埠工程師	Contractor	承包商
Promulgate	頒布		

二十、固體廢棄物（垃圾）（Solid Waste）——Within MARPOL Annex V Special Areas

a. Disposal into the sea of the following is prohibited: all plastics, including but not limited to *synthetic ropes*, plastic garbage bags and incinerator ashes from plastic products which may contain toxic or heavy metal residues, and all other garbage, including paper products, rags, glass, metal, bottles, *crockery*, *dunnage*, lining and packing materials.

b. When garbage is mixed with other discharges having different disposal or discharge requirements, the more stringent requirements shall apply.

c. Except as provided in paragraph 1.c, food wastes, either ground our unground, shall only be discharged outside 12 nautical miles from the nearest land.

d. Discharges of food waste must be made while the ship is *proceeding en route*. En route means that vessels shall be underway and *making way*, on a course that spreads the discharge as much as practicable.

e. *Incinerators* may be used per Section 5 of this chapter. Incinerator ash may not be disposed of at sea while in a Special Area.

f. *Equipment casualties* that either threaten or result in a discharge of plastics shall be reported through the prescribed Product Line casualty reporting system. The initial report shall note the potential for discharge and list Commandant (CG-452) as an addressee. The commencement, duration and amount of such discharges of plastics shall be reported to the appropriate operational commander.

g. If any type of garbage, other than food waste, must be discharged due to special operational circumstances that impact the health, safety, and sanitation of the crew and cutter, in addition to the record keeping requirements detailed in B.1.c of the chapter, an official message detailing the location, amount, type and reason for this discharge must be reported to Commandants (CG-751), (CG-452), (CG-0941E), and their operational commander within 72 hours of the discharge.

Synthetic ropes	塑膠繩	**Crockery**	陶器
Dunnage	襯料	**Proceeding en route**	在航行途中盡行
Making way	前往	**Incinerators**	焚化爐
Equipment casualties	設備損毀		

二十一、壓艙水與錨系統底泥之控管（Ship Ballast Water and Anchor System Sediment Control）——US Coast Guard Policy

1. **Ballasting.**

   All vessels capable of conducting ballast operations shall do so in accordance with their *Damage Control Books* (*DCB*). Vessels that ballast their fuel tanks (not *segregated ballast tanks*) should treat the ballast water taken aboard as an "oily mixture". Ballasting and deballasting shall be conducted in a manner to minimize the introduction of *nonnative species*.

All ballasting and de-ballasting evolutions shall be as indicated below:

a. Record in the Machinery Log each transfer of ballast water noting ships location, water depth, tanks involved, and amount of ballast taken aboard or discharged.

b. Avoid the discharge or uptake of ballast water in areas within or that may directly affect *marine sanctuaries*, *marine preserves*, marine parks, or *coral reefs*.

c. Minimize or avoid uptake of ballast water in the following areas or situations:

(1) Areas known to have *infestations* or *populations* of *harmful organisms* or *pathogens* (e.g., toxic algal blooms).

(2) Areas near *sewage outfalls*.

(3) Areas near *dredging operations*.

(4) Areas where *tidal flushing* is known to be poor or at times when tidal flow is known to be more turbid.

(5) In darkness when *bottom-dwelling organisms* may rise up in the *water column*.

(6) Where propellers may stir up the *sediment*.

(7) Areas with *pods of whales*, *convergence zones*, and *boundaries of major currents*.

2. **Ballast Water Management Plan.**

All vessels capable of conducting ballast operations shall develop and maintain a *vessel-specific* ballast water management plan that allows those responsible for the plan's implementation to understand and follow the vessel's ballast water management strategy.

3. **Vessels with segregated ballast tanks.**

If your vessel carries ballast water that was taken on in areas less than 200 nautical miles from any shore into the waters of the U.S.

after operating beyond the EEZ, one of the following ballast water management practices must be employed while adhering to your DC Book:

a. Perform a complete ballast water exchange in an area no less than 200 nautical miles from any shore prior to discharging ballast water into U.S. waters. To ensure a minimum of 95% ballast water exchange, ballast tanks shall be flushed a minimum of three times.

b. Discharge ballast water to an approved *receiving facility*.

c. If unable to meet (a) or (b) then retain ballast water as long as safely practicable or conduct flushing as far from shore as possible.

4. **Vessels without segregated ballast tanks.**

Vessels that ballast fuel tanks shall meet all of the requirements listed for segregated ballast tanks. In addition, and to the maximum extent practicable, fuel tanks shall be de-ballasted using an OWS equipped with a functioning, *calibrated* oil content meter (OCM).

Damage Control Books	損害管制簿	Segregated ballast tanks	隔離壓載艙
Non-native species	外來物種	Marine sanctuaries	海洋保護區
Marine preserves	海洋保育區	Coral reefs	珊瑚礁
Infestation	感染	Population	群
Harmful organisms	有害生物	Pathogens	病原體
Sewage outfalls	汙水放流	Dredging operation	濬渫施作
Tidal flushing	潮水沖洗	Bottom-dwelling organisms	底棲生物
Water column	水團	Sediment	底泥
Pods of whales	鯨魚群	Convergence zones	輻和帶
Boundaries of major currents	主要洋流邊界	Vessel-specific	該船專屬
Receiving facility	收受設施	Calibrated	經過校正的

二十二、保護海洋自然生物（Marine Wildlife Protection）

1. 鯨魚（Whales）

a. Lookouts shall be especially alert to whales *unexpectedly surfacing* within 100 yards of the vessel.

b. In the event of a whale unexpectedly surfacing within 100 yards of the vessel, take action as *prudent* and appropriate to ensure the safety of both the crew and the whale and to minimize damage to the vessel.

c. In areas of known whale *migration routes* (e.g. southeast Alaska or Mid-Atlantic coast) or high animal density (e.g. San Juan Islands area or Cape Cod) be aware of local conditions and especially alert for activity.

d. Do not approach whales head on during non-emergency maneuvering. Avoid North Atlantic or North Pacific Right Whales by 500 yards and all other whale species by 100 yards, except when assisting in an animal rescue effort or enforcing the Marine Mammal or Endangered Species Act.

2. 噪音（Noise）——US Coast Guard Policy

a. Workplace noise.

b. Workplace noise is not environmental noise. Abatement of workplace noise is addressed in Chapter 4 of The Safety and Environmental Health Manual, COMDTINST M5100.47 (series).

c. Noise Generating Devices.

d. The use of powered tools, machinery, outboard loudspeakers or any other devices that emit excessive noise, either directly or indirectly, shall be restricted to normal daylight working hours to the *maximum possible extent*.

e. Cavitations. Most (83%) of the *acoustic field* surrounding large vessels is the result of propeller cavitation (when air spaces created by the motion of propellers collapse). When ships *cavitate*, relatively little acoustic energy is transmitted into the water from on-board machinery or movement of the vessel through the water. Given that acoustic energy radiated into water by transiting ships represents wasted energy that could be used to more efficiently propel the ship, making modifications may have the dual benefit of reducing *radiated noise* and reducing vessel-operating costs. Further, vessels fitted for reduced radiation of underwater sound also tend to be quieter onboard, which is desirable for the crew. Optimal quieting is achieved when this goal is incorporated into the design of vessels and strictly adhered to during construction.

Unexpectedly surfacing	非預期浮出水面	Prudent	謹慎的
Migration route	遷徙路徑	Maximum possible extent	最大可能情況
Acoustic field	聲場	Cavitate	空蝕
Radiated noise	輻射噪音		

第二章　口說輪機
（Speaking Marine Engineering）

　　英語在輪機工作當中，使用最多的可能就是以口說的方式。當船靠港時，常有像是加油船、代理行、零件經銷商、岸上維修人員等需要溝通、協調。平時航行當中，更不可避免需要和同船、同部門的同事溝通，以交接任務和完成工作。無奈，這對於一位輪機員來說，往往正是最困難的部分。本章大部分內容為輪機員在機艙各種情境下，可能進行的一些對話，請讀者練習、熟悉之。

第一節　這要多久？（How Long Will It Take?）

　　時間，對於一個輪機員而言，往往是很重要的考量。所以在許多情況下，「究竟要多久？」往往也就成了最常問的問題。以下會話，應有助於幫助您在某場合當中，妥適的提出和回答這個問題。例如日常工作中，以下便是很常用到的句子：

A同事：I usually drive to work. It takes me about twenty minutes.

B同事：I usually walk to work. It takes me about forty minutes.

　　又例如，當一位三管輪（4/E）在機艙遇上一位駐埠工程師（Port Engineer）時，便有可能針對燃油濾器和燃油淨油機，產生以下對話：

Port Engineer: How long will it take to clean the fuel oil filter?

4/E: It usually takes me about 10 minutes to get it done.

Port Engineer: How long will it take to do regular maintenance on the fuel oil purifier?

4/E: Well, that usually takes me more than an hour to get everything done. But it takes much shorter if I got helper working with me.

第二節　在美國用早餐（Breakfast in the States）

　　假使你有機會在美國某港口下船或上船，碰巧需要在旅館休息一晚，次日一早在餐廳用餐，遇到服務生Janet，便有可能用上以下對話。記得，走前可要留小費在桌上！

場景：輪機實習生阿元（*Yuan (Y) is served by a waitress Janet (J) in the restaurant of a hotel.*）

J: Good morning, I am Janet, may I take your order?

Y: Yah! Sure!

J: What would you like for breakfast?

Y: I'll take an American breakfast, please.

J: Well, how do you want your eggs, and what kind of toast?

Y: I'd like two eggs, *wheat*, *hash-browns* and a cup of coffee. (I'll have two eggs, wheat toast, sausage and coffee please!)

J: How would you like your eggs?

Y: I'll have it *sunny side up*. (I'll have *scrambled eggs*. / I'll have *poached eggs*, please. / I'll have my eggs *hard boiled*. / I'll have my *eggs over easy*.)

J: What kind of toast would you like?

Y: I'd like wheat. (I'd like white toast. / I'd like rye bread.)

J: Sausage or bacon?

Y: Bacon, please.

J: What kind of coffee would you like?

Y: I'd like a cup of regular coffee please.

J: What kind of milk would you like?

Y: I'd like *whole milk*, please!

Y: *Check please*!

Wheat	小麥（吐司）	Hard boiled	煮到全熟
Hash-browns	煎馬鈴薯餅	Eggs over easy	半生蛋
Sunny side up	半生荷包蛋	Whole milk	全脂牛奶
Scrambled eggs	炒蛋	Check please	買單
Poached eggs	白煮蛋		

第三節　運轉情況報告（Reporting for Operating Condition）

一、報告溫度壓力和測深（Briefing on Temperatures, Pressures and Soundings）

The ○○ (equipment) temperature minimum/maximum is ○○ degrees (centigrade).

Maintain ○○ degrees (centigrade) above / below normal temperature.

Do not exceed a minimum/maximum temperature of ○○ degrees (centigrade).

The ○○ (equipment) pressure minimum/maximum is ○○ bars.

Maintain ○○ bars above / below normal pressure.

Do not exceed a pressure of ○○ bars.

Ballast / Fresh water / Fuel / Oil / Slop sounding is ○○ metres / cubic metres.

Sounding of ○○ side No. ○○ cargo tank is ○○ metres / cubic metres. No. ○○ cargo hold is ○○ centimetres.

二、針對主機與輔機的運轉提出報告（Briefing on Operation of Main Engine and Auxiliary Equipment）

Present revolution of the main engine is ○○ per minute.

Present output of the main engine / auxiliary engine is ○○ kiloWatt.

Present pitch of the propeller is ○○... degrees.

There's no problem with main engine.

There's problem with main engine / auxiliary engine.

Call the Watch Engineer, if the problems continue.

Call the Duty Engineer ○○ minutes before the arrival at ○○.

三、針對泵送燃油、壓艙水等提出報告（Briefing on Pumping of Fuel, Ballast Water, etc.）

There is no pumping at present.

We are filling / We filled (No.) ○○ double bottom tank(s) / the ballast tanks / the ○○ tank(s).

Fill up ○○ tones to the alarm point.

We are discharging / We discharged (No.) ○○ from double bottom tank(s) / the ballast tanks / the ○○ tank(s).

We are transferring / We transferred fuel / ballast / fresh water / oil from (No.) ○○ tank(s) to (No.) ○○ tank(s).

We require a further generator to operate an additional ballast pump.

四、就特殊機器狀況和修理提出報告（Briefing on Special Machinery Events and Repairs）

註：以下文中 UTC (Coordinated Universal Time) 爲世界標準時間。

There was a breakdown of the main engine at UTC from ○○ to ○○.

There was a breakdown of ○○ (at ○○○○ UTC / from ○○ to ○○ UTC).

There was a total blackout (at ○○ UTC / from ○○ to ○○ UTC).

There was a blackout in ○○ (at ○○ UTC / from ○○ to ○○ UTC).

Main engine was stopped (at ○○ UTC / from ○○ to ○○ UTC) due to ○○.

Speed was reduced (at ○○ UTC / from ○○ to ○○ UTC) due to ○○.

Call the Master / Chief Engineer if the revolutions of the main engine is below ○○ per minute.

Call the Master / Chief Engineer / Watch Engineer if ○○.

Check the pumps / emergency generator and report.

(Bilge) pump(s) in ○○ / emergency generator is / are operational.

○○ is / are not operational (yet).

○○ will be operational in ○○ minutes.

五、供電（Check the Power Supply and Report）

Power (in / at) ○○ is available.

○○ is not available (yet).

○○ will be available in ○○ minutes.

六、損害管制設備（Check the Damage Control Equipment and Report）

All damage control equipment is complete and available.

Damage control equipment is not complete.

Complete the damage control equipment.

七、泵的運轉（Operating Pumping Equipment）——Phrases for communication with bunker barge / oil terminal

What is the (maximum) loading rate / discharge rate?

The (maximum) loading rate / discharge rate is: ○○ tones per hour.

Is the *crude oil washing* (*COW*) *system* / *inert gas system* (*IGS*) operational?

Yes, the COW system / inert gas system is operational.

No, the COW system / inert gas system is not operational (yet).

The COW system / inert gas will be operational in ○○ minutes.

When will crude oil washing start?

Crude oil washing will start in ○○ minutes.

八、泵送壓力（What is the Pumping Pressure?）

The pumping pressure is ○○ bar.

Can we connect the loading arm?

Yes, you can connect the loading arm.

No, you cannot connect the loading arm (yet).

Connect the loading arm in ○○ minutes.

Inform ○○ minutes before loading / discharge will start / finish.

Loading / Discharge will start / finish in ○○ minutes.

九、油艙惰性氣體處理（Inert Gas Treatment for Oil Tanks）

Are your tanks *inerted*?

Yes, my tanks are inerted.

No, my tanks are not inerted (yet).

My tanks will be inerted in ○○ minutes.

What is the pressure in the inerted tanks?

The pressure in the inerted tanks is ○○ bar.

十、裝卸貨油（Loading / Discharging Cargo Oil）

Are the cargo hoses / *booms* connected?

Yes, the cargo hoses / booms are connected.

No, the cargo hoses / booms are not connected (yet).

The cargo hoses / booms will be connected in ○○ minutes.

Are the cargo hoses / booms disconnected?

Yes, the cargo hoses / booms are disconnected.

No, the cargo hoses / booms are not disconnected (yet).

The cargo hoses / booms will be disconnected in ○○ minutes.

Are you ready to load /discharge?

Yes, I am ready to load / discharge.

No, I am not ready to load /discharge (yet).

I will be ready to load / discharge in ○○ minutes.

Keep a safe working pressure.

Open the valve(s) and report.

All full open aboard / ashore.

Close the valve(s) and report.

All full closed aboard / ashore.

Start pumping (slowly).

Are you pumping / receiving?

Yes, I am pumping / receiving.

No, I am not pumping / not receiving.

Increase / Decrease pumping rate to ○○ revolutions / bar.

Quantity of ○○ tones received, stop pumping.

第四節　滑油泵切換使用（The Switch for the Lube Oil Pump）

場景：*Cadet Yuan (Y) and Second Engineer (2/E) are standing by the main engine lubricating oil pumps.*

2/E: Come up here Yuan, do you know them?

Y: No, I don't know. What are they?

2/E: This lubricating pump is for *exhaust valve* lubrication and that's for *rocker arm*.

Y: Are they *motor-driven*?

2/E: Correct.

Y: Is this the switch for them?

2/E: Do you remember the switch box fitted over the maneuvering handle?

Y: Oh, right, I remember that.

2/E: Let's go down to the lower floor. This switch is of the three-way type, OFF, MANUAL, and AUTOMATIC.

Y: How do they work?

2/E: If you put it at MANUAL and press the botton, two motors begin to start at once. And if you put it OFF, they stop.

Y: What about the AUTO, then?

2/E: When it's at automatic, the pump motors don't always begin to start. Here's an *interlock*.

Y: I see. If so, can we always keep the switch at automatic?

2/E: Yes, but during the cooling right after the FWE, you'd better turn it off.

Y: Why so?

2/E: We sure don't want to supply too much lube-oil to the exhaust valve when ergine is stop.

Exhaust valve	排氣閥	Motor-driven	馬達驅動
Rocker arm	搖臂	Interlock	互鎖

第五節　滑油泵的構造（The Construction of Lube Oil Pump）

場景：*Cadet Yuan (Y) and Second Engineer (2/E) are standing by the main engine lubricating oil pumps.*

2/E: Do you want to know the *features* of this lube oil pump.

Y: Sure, would you explain to me?

2/E: Look at here, the oil suction. At the top, a small *nozzle tip* is fitted, and under the nozzle a plate valve and two pingpong balls are provided. We call it the *float suction*.

Y: The float suction?

2/E: Yah, lubricant run when there's enough *head difference* between the oil tank and the pump.

Y: I see.

2/E: So, when the oil level comes up and up, two pingpong balls begin to float up and push the plate valve.

Y: Interesting! Let me guess, when the oil comes up to the certain level, the valve tends to close the nozzle.

2/E: Correct! Very good Yuan! There's the *pressure adjusting screw* under the cap nut. It should be always full close.

Y: How come?

2/E: This lube pump is the *intermittent type* but not the continuous feed type. Lubricant is fed every about 12 minutely interval and between the *feeding intervals*, lubricant is bypassed.

Y: Okay.

2/E: Look at this button, Yuan. We call it the instant feed button. If keep pushing it, lubricant is fed continuously.

Y: I see. How much is the proper feeding amount of lubricant?

2/E: It can be adjusted in four steps by the *adjusting cams* fitted inside the pump.

Y: I understand. Thank you very much for the teach, sir.

Features	功能	Intermittent type	間歇型
Nozzle tip	噴嘴頭	Feeding intervals	供油間隔
Float suction	吸入浮子	Adjusting cams	調節凸輪
Pressure adjusting screw	壓力調節螺絲		

第六節　掃氣道與輔鼓風機（Scavenging Air Trunk and Auxiliary Blower）

場景：*Cadet Yuan (Y) and Second Engineer (2/E) are standing by the scavenging trunk.*

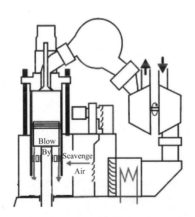

2/E: Look Yuan, this big chamber is the scavenging air trunk. The interior is divided into two *compartments*. There're *check valves* fitted between them.

Y: What type of check valve is it used? Is it a *Harmonica type*?

2/E: It has been the Harmonica valve long time ago. Now it's the solid plate valve.

Y: Oh, I see.

2/E: The supercharged engine drives auxiliary blowers during the low loads.

Y: Because of low in air supply in low loads?

2/E: Correct, Yuan. Let's set the blower's switch "ON", before we start the engine. It's at "AUTO" position.

Y: What is the *sensing signal* for the auto-start-stop?

2/E: It's the scavenging air pressure.

Y: For what interval, shall we clean the inside of scavenging air trunk?

2/E: It should be cleaned about every half a year.

Compartments	空間	Harmonica type	口琴型
Check valves	止回閥	Sensing signal	感測信號

第七節　氣缸注油器（Cylinder Oil Lubricator）

場景：*Standing next to main engine, the Third Engineer (3/E) is teaching the cadet Yuan (Y) about some routine practice of the cylinder oil lubricator.*

3/E: Look here Yuan, this is the cylinder oil lubricator.

Y: Oh, yes. Can you teach me how I can control the amount of oil supply?

3/E: There're two ways. The one is by this level handle, and the other, by this adjusting screw.

Y: Yes, Third.

3/E: The normal position of this lever is *horizontal.* If you want to increase the amount of oil supply, set the lever at lower side. And the other way for reducing the oil supply.

Y: I see. Is it all right to keep it horizontal?

3/E: Yes, But if the arrival or departure time is very long, you'd better set it at the lowest.

Y: What case would that be?

3/E: Such as when ship is passing through a *narrow channel* or under foggy condition.

Y: All right.

3/E: Well, when you want to control the oil supply *individually*, you must re-adjust by this screw. The stroke of each *plunger* is therefore changed.

Y: I see.

3/E: See the scale, Yuan? There are 6 horizontal lines, this is so called position 5A.

Y: Is that so?

3/E: Turn the screw *a quarter* into anti-clockwise will be the 5B. Another quarter is 5C. Try yourself, Yuan.

Y: Like this?

3/E: Yah, it is the 5D, another quarter.

Y: Right, more quarter.

3/E: Now, it reaches just one turn, so, it arrived at the A.

Y : I see. Thank you so much, Third.

Horizontal	水平	Individually	個別的
Narrow channel	狹窄水道	Plunger	柱塞

第八節　機艙中輪機員對話

主機備便準備開航（Preparing to Sail）

場景：在一艘柴油機船的機艙，大管輪（2/E）帶著剛上船的新科三管
　　　輪（4/E），一同進行開船前的準備工作，包括冷卻水、滑油、
　　　啟動空氣和電力等等。輪機實習生阿元（Y）在一旁學習、幫
　　　忙，接著輪機長（C/E）也來到控制室。

　　同學們可以分別扮演大管輪、三管輪、機匠和輪機長練習對話，接
著也可以互換角色，再反覆練習。

C/E: The ship is scheduled to leave Keelung at six o'clock.

2/E: Okay, let's start the preparation for sea.

（冷卻淡水情況如何？）

4/E: The *circulating pump* is started. How about the water tank, Yuan?

Y: I've just checked the fresh water *expansion tank.* It's full.

2/E: Good.

4/E: Are we going to use system No.1 for this voyage?

2/E: Right, let's use No.1. And how do you set No.2 pump in stand-by condition, Yuan?

Y: Well, I'll first make sure the suction and delivery valves of both pumps are open. Then I'll switch on the *NFB* of the No. 1 pump and start it. And then I'll switch on the NFB of the stand-by pump and turn the change-over switch to the stand-by side.

2/E: Good, you need to *observe this sequence strictly.*

4/E: Let's get rid of air in the system.

Y: Okay, right away.

2/E: Now, heat up the water system to around 55℃ by the time of the engine trial.

Y: Yes, I'll do it.

（潤滑油情況如何？）

4/E: I've just checked lubricating *oil sumps.*

2/E: All right. Start up the lubricating pumps for both main system and supercharger.

4/E: They are now operating. Delivery and suction pressures are good and oil is flowing uniformly from all the bearings.

2/E: Good. It's not necessary this time, but if the lubricating oil has been undisturbed in the drain tank for quite a while, a *sample* should be *drawn* from the bottom to check that there is no *sediment* or water before starting up the pump.

Y: This must be one of important procedures before running the engine.

2/E: Now you can *put in the turning gear.* Are the *cylinder mechanical*

lubricators ready, Yuan?

Y: Yes, they are. I've *replenished* them already.

2/E: Okay. Then check they work correctly by hand.

Y: Looks good, sir. Cylinder oil is flowing at all *sight glasses*.

2/E: Good. Are all indicator valves open and is *maneuvering handle* in the stop position, Third?

4/E: Yes, all are set, sir.

2/E: Okay. Give the engine a turn. Also you may want to check that no water is leaking into the *crankcase, scavenge air belt* or from the any other parts.

4/E: All good, Sir.

（啟動空氣如何？）

2/E: What is the pressure in the starting *air reservoirs,* third?

4/E: It's 23kg (*kg/cm²*), sir.

2/E: Go ahead pump them up to their maximum pressure.

Y: Should the fuel oil system be *primed*?

4/E: Yah, go ahead start up the priming pump and try to clear air out of the system.

2/E: Make sure the temperature is correct.

4/E: Everything seems okay.

2/E: Well, how much time do we have now?

（這時，輪機長進到了控制室）

4/E: It's five thirty, thirty minutes before standby.

2/E: All right, it's time the fuel injection valves need cooling water.

4/E: Yes, they are all in operation.

（電力供應如何？）

2/E: Everything is fine. Let's start No.3 generator and *put it in parallel* with the other two.

4/E: Yes, three generators are running in parallel.

2/E: Okay, let's stop turning and take out the turning gear. Call the bridge to give the engine telegraph a test.

Y: Turning gear disengaged and *telegraph test* done, sir.

2/E: Okay, open the starting air stop valve.

4/E: The valve is open. Water and *impurity* drained.

2/E: Give a test to the *reversing and control gear* before putting on the starting air.

C/E: Be sure that all alarms and monitors are on. Set the *telegraph logger* on.

（這時俥鐘響起，同時顯示「*Standby Engine*」）

2/E: Stand-by engine!

C/E: Answer back to the bridge and we are ready to go.

Circulating pump	循環泵	**Maneuvering handle**	操俥桿
Expansion tank	膨脹櫃	**Crankcase**	曲軸箱
NFB	無熔絲開關（Non-fuse breaker）	**Scavenge air belt**	掃氣道
Observe this sequence strictly	嚴格遵照此順序	**Air reservoirs**	儲氣槽
Oil sumps	油池	**kg/cm²**	Kilogram per square centimeter
Sample drawn	採樣	**Primed**	引注
Sediment	沉澱物	**Put it in parallel**	並聯運轉
Put in the turning gear	接上轉俥機	**Telegraph test**	車鐘測試
Cylinder mechanical lubricators	氣缸注油器	**Impurity**	雜質
Replenished	補充	**Reversing and control gear**	倒俥與控制裝置
Sight glasses	窺視鏡	**Telegraph logger**	俥鐘記錄器

第九節 調整主機燃油泵之設定（Adjustment of Main Engine Fuel Pump Setting）

場景：*Standing on 2^(nd) level of main engine, the Third Engineer (3/E) is teaching the cadet (Yuan, Y) about some routine practice of the fuel pump*

3/E: Look here, Yuan! This is the *crank angle* marked on the *flywheel*. As this point is No.3 cylinder's *top dead center*, the *injection timing* is now at 8 degrees before TDC.

Y: Oh yes. I see.

3/E: Go ahead check the injection timing of every cylinder in the same way.

Y: Yes, thanks. But, how can I readjust the timing?

3/E: Suppose you are going to readjust the timing of No.2 cylinder's fuel pump, at first, turn the engine and top it at 9 degrees before top of No.3 cylinder. See the position on flywheel? See that?

Y: Yah, right.

3/E: Then, come up to the fuel pump side and loosen this nut and readjust the adjusting bolt until the line on the plunger guide *coincides* perfectly with the line on the window of housing. Try it.

Y: Yes.

3/E: That's all right. You may secure the nut firmly after done.

Y: All right, Sir.

Crank angle	曲軸角	Injection timing	噴燃正時
Flywheel	飛輪	Coincides	對齊
Top dead center	上死點（TDC）		

第十節 空氣冷卻器與濕氣分離器（Air Cooler and Moisture Separator）

場景：*Standing on 2nd level of main engine, the Third Engineer (3/E) is teaching the cadet (Yuan, Y) about some routine practice of the air cooler*

3/E: Yuan, let's go to 2nd level of the starboard side.

Y: Oh, yes.

3/E: As you know, the compressed air sent from the blower of turbo-charger passes through this cooler and is cooled.

Y: If it's cooled too much, a lot of moisture *will be born*.

3/E: Correct! That's why a water separator is attached under the air cooler in order to catch water before getting into the cylinders.

Y: Sorry, I can't find the separator?

3/E: See this? Here are two *branches* connected to the main pipe. Keep this stop valve a half open. Well, actually, just a little bit open.

Y: Okay, will do.

Will be born	產生	Branches	分叉、支路

第十一節 水質檢驗（Testing Water）

場景：*Second Engineer (2/E) and Third Engineer (3/E) are entering the water test room on the second floor of the engine room.*

2/E: Here's where we do our *water test* job for boiler water and cooling water.

3/E: It sure equips with everything needed.

2/E: Yah, it has almost all *testing kits* and *chemicals* we need for the test.

3/E: It's a nice looking box.

2/E: It is what we call "*universal tester*". It contains all testing kits for measuring pH value, *chloride, hardness,* and *phosphate ion.*

3/E: And those are the chemicals.

2/E: Right! See the cock fitted above the left side basin?

3/E: Yah, what's it for?

2/E: They are for taking boiler water samples. Just turn the cocks and you'll have a cooled water sample.

3/E: Wow, what a convenient water sampler.

2/E: Sure it is. Now, these two books are for water test record. All readings are to be *plotted against* the design *curve.*

3/E: Well, it's a little different form from what I had before.

2/E: You'll soon get used to it. And this is the chemical record book. *Remaining quantities* of all chemicals and *apparatus* are checked every seven days and the results are filled in here.

3/E: Yah, that's about the same as I had before.

2/E: Great!

3/E: Oh yah, how often do we need to do the boiler water test?

2/E: Everyday. Well, why don't you take some boiler water samples to give it a try?

3/E: Yes, ⋯. Is this good enough?

2/E: Yah, good enough. First we are going to determine *alkalinity* to *phenol-phthalein*. To test for *acidity* in boiler water, we use *litmus paper*.

3/E: Is this the filter paper, Sir?

2/E: Yes, use a *china beaker* when the sample is filtered.

3/E: Well, thanks so much for the instruction.

Water test	水質試驗	**Remaining quantities**	餘存量
Testing kits	檢測組	**Apparatus**	器材
Chemicals	化學藥品	**Alkalinity**	鹼度
Universal tester	萬用檢測器	**Phenol-phthalein**	酚酞
Chloride	氯化合物	**Acidity**	酸度
Hardness	水硬度	**Litmus paper**	石蕊試紙
Phosphate ion	磷酸鹽	**China beaker**	磁燒杯
Plotted against curve	畫點在曲線上		

第十二節　排氣閥挺桿間隙（Tappet Clearance of Exhaust Valve）

場景：*In the engine room of a ship staying in port. Third Engineer (3/E) is about to adjust for tappet clearance of exhaust valves of a diesel generator. Cadet (Yuan, Y) is leaning and helping.*

Y: Will you teach me to adjust the tappet clearance of exhaust valve?

輪機英文

3/E: Okay, sure.

Y: Thank you.

3/E: At first, you must operate the lube pump and keep oil pressure around 3.0 to 3.5 kg/cm^2.

Y: Okay, but could you tell me why I need to operate lube pump?

3/E: Because on the *roller guide* of exhaust valve, the cushion is provided for lowering the moving force and noise of the *drive mechanism.*

Y: Right, I see.

3/E: Let's go down there.

Y: Yes.

3/E: This is turning gear. Turn the switch of the *turning motor* on, Yuan?

Y: All right, it's on now.

3/E: You must turn the engine and stop it at the top dead center of which the tappet clearance is going to be adjusted.

Y: Why is that, sir?

3/E: Because it is where the crank angle is accepted unless the roller is on the lift of cam.

Y: I see. Thank you so much for the teach, sir.

Roller guide	滾輪導塊	Turning motor	轉俥馬達
Drive mechanism	驅動機制		

第十三節　主配電盤例行檢查（Regular Checkup on a Main Switchboard）

場景：*Standing by main switchboard, the Third Engineer (3/E) is teaching the cadet (Yuan, Y) about some regular checkup.*

Y: Can you teach me about regular routine checkups to the main switchboard?

3/E: Of course. We first examine the contact surface of the *air circuit breakers*. It is very important to maintain the best contact so the voltage drop can be kept at minimum.

Y: Is it okay that I *file* the contact surface if it is *roughened*?

3/E: You'd better use finest sand paper and not to file it unless serious burning has taken place.

Y: Yes, I understand.

3/E: Make sure all screws and nuts are tight. Loss of tension could result in sparking overheating.

Y: Yah, I remember that! Once overheated, its effect is *cumulative* and may rapidly lead to complete failure.

3/E: Right. Also make sure the lock nuts are all tightened. You should held one nut by a *spanner* and other tightened against it with another spanner.

Y: All right. I'll do that.

3/E: Good, and keep in mind safety is always the first priority.

Y: Right, safety comes first.

Air circuit breakers	空氣斷路器	Cumulative	累積
File	剉	Spanner	板手
Roughened	變粗、粗糙		

第十四節　電機的故障和修理（Faults and Repairs on Electrical Machinery）

場景：*Standing by main switchboard, Second Engineer (2/E) and Third Engineer (3/E) are about to work on some electrical machineries.*

2/E: Any idea for today, third?

3/E: Well, I have to find out the cause of the *defective motor*. And there're some routing adjustment and checkup with the main switchboard. Also I'd like to clean the D.C. generator for the *emergency battery*, if time remains.

2/E: Defective motor?

3/E: Yah, it's for A/C cooling water. It failed last night.

2/E: I would say it's because of the *starter* rather than the motor itself.

3/E: Right, that's quite possible. I sure will check it thoroughly. And I might renew the bearings. They do make unusual noise recently.

2/E: Oh, about the switchboard, be sure to *make live parts dead* first before opening the door.

3/E: Yah, right, thanks much for remind. It *cannot be emphasized too much* that care should be taken.

2/E: Will you tell me the results when you finish the jobs?

3/E: Sure, I'll report everything to you once I get it done.

Defective motor	故障馬達	Make live parts dead	使動不了
Emergency battery	緊急電瓶	Cannot be emphasized too much	太重要了
Starter	啟動器		

第十五節　直流發電機保養（Maintenance on D.C. Generator）

場景：*Standing by a DC generator, the Third Engineer (3/E) is teaching the cadet (Yuan, Y) about some regular maintenance.*

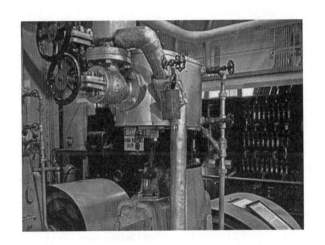

3/E: Yuan, let's check the *commutator*. It is totally enclosed. Can you see that?

Y: Yes, I see it. The doors need to be removed to see all *brush arms* and commutator.

3/E: Then, let's open the covers. Check to see if the *water-tight gasket* is damaged.

Y: There! The cover removed and now we can see inside.

3/E: How's the *commutation*?

Y: Not so good, sir. Scaring *sparking* shows around the brush contact surface. I guess it needs some cleaning and polishing.

3/E: Right. Stop the machine to give it a thorough checkup.

Y: All connections inside checked. There are several *faults*.

輪機英文

3/E: What are they?

Y: A number of brushes are sticking in their boxes and the *commutator* has a roughened surface caused by sparking.

3/E: Let's see, the *rigding* is *excessive*. Also the brush rocker is *slacked off*. Some of the *micas* show signs of *projecting above the segments*.

Y: Oh, look at this. The *ventilating duct* is *clogged* with dirt.

3/E: It seems to me that all these *defects* together cause the sparking. Anyway let's go ahead clean and polish the roughened surface with *smooth glass paper*.

Y: Yes. I'll do it.

Commutator	整流器	Slacked off	鬆掉
Brush arms	碳刷臂	Micas	雲母
Water-tight gasket	水密墊片	Projecting above segments	凸出邊緣
Commutation	換向	Ventilating duct	通風管
Sparking	產生火花	Clogged	堵塞
Faults	瑕疵	Defects	毛病
Rigding excessive	過度凸起	Smooth glass paper	細砂紙

第十六節　船抵達美國西雅圖（Arrival in Port Seattle）

場景：由於船即將到港，包括輪機長*(C/E)*、大管輪*(2/E)*、二管輪*(3/ E)*和三管輪*(4/E)*等輪機人員，都在機艙中忙著備便。駕駛台 *(Bridge, B)*也參與對話。

（電話鈴聲響起，三管輪接電話）

4/E: Engine control room.

B: Hello, this is the Third Officer speaking. Our ship is now twenty miles from the port. She is expected to arrive at the entrance about one hour later. The *pilot* will join us there.

4/E: All right, Third Officer. Thanks for your information.

（三管輪拿起電話聽筒並撥號給輪機長）

4/E: Good morning, Chief. This is control room. We received the information from the bridge that stand-by will be rung for entering port about one hour from now. We are going to *commence* the preparations.

C/E: Thank you for the call.

3/E: Let's do it. We need to switch the fuel oil from C oil to A oil for *maneuvering*. So go and read the fuel flow meter when I signal. Watch carefully both thermometer and indicator of the *automatic viscosity regulator* and close the steam inlet valve when diesel oil starts to flow inside.

4/E: Okay, here we go.

（三管輪回到控制室）

4/E: The *flow meter* reading, 23705. And now it's time to shut off heating steam. Fuel changed and all *related valves* closed.

3/E: All right. Then we are going to reduce the engine revolution gradually to the Harbor Full Ahead.

（大管輪進到控制室）

2/E: Hi, how are things going?

4/E: We've just changed fuel oil. Now we are about to reduce revolutions.

2/E: Okay, watch the *critical speed zone*. Pass it quickly. The revolutions must be reduced gradually, though.

4/E: Yes, I'll do my best.

（電話響起，同時接到「距領港站5海里」（*Five miles before the pilot station*）的通知）

2/E: How about the cooling sea water return temperature? Pay close attention to it and try to adjust the hot valve if the temperature tends to fall.

4/E: The revolutions are set in Harbor Full.

（輪機長進到控制室）

2/E: The Bridge just informed us of five miles before the pilot station, Chief.

C/E: They gave a ring to my office, too. Well, how're all preparations works going?

2/E: Yes, sir. Three generators are *operating in parallel*. The standby No. 2 air compressor is operating in parallel with No. 1 to fill up the *air reservoirs*. The starting system is now opened and other equipments required for standby are all ready.

C/E: That' good. Well, how are those temperatures?

2/E: All good, sir. Also, fuel oil and cooling water return temperatures are maintained.

C/E: All right, then, leave the maneuvering of the main engine to the Third Engineer. He should be familiarized with the procedure.

（三管輪回到控制室）

2/E: Take the maneuvering handle, Third. Stand-by will be rung any second.

4/E: There it is. Stand by engine, Sir!

2/E: Answer back to the bridge. Get ready to reduce the revolutions!

4/E: Stop engine!

2/E: Check the cooling sea water return temperature. Stop the sea water pump when necessary.

（俥鐘響起同時顯示「用俥結束」（FWE））

4/E: *Finished with engine.*

3/E: Air stop valves shut off and all *indicator valves* are open now!

2/E: Shift the maneuvering handle to the START position and keep it there until the air runs out.

4/E: Yes, Sir.... Air running is now over. The maneuvering handle is in its stop position.

2/E: Okay, put in the turning gear and commence the turning. Remember to turn the cylinder lubricators.

C/E: All right, folks, let's work on the crankcase inspection while the engine is turning.

2/E: Yes, it's time to open crankcase doors.

（三管輪回到控制室）

4/E: All crankcase doors opened, sir.

C/E: Okay, let's give a thorough checkup to all working parts. All the faults must be made good before we sail.

（大管輪也回到控制室）

2/E: All checkups done and everything look good.

4/E: Cooling water systems shut down.

3/E: Fuel booster pump stopped.

2/E: Good. I wonder whether there is something forgotten. Well, let me see,...... Oh, better stop the *ventilators* and close the *skylight* since it is cold and snowy outside

Pilot	領港	**Operating in parallel**	並聯運轉
Commence	開始進行	**Air reservoirs**	儲氣槽
maneuvering	動俥	**Finished with Engine**	用俥結束（*FWE*）
Automatic viscosity regulator	黏度自動調節器	**Indicator valves**	示功閥
Flow meter	流量表	**Ventilators**	通風
Related valves	相關閥	**Skylight**	天窗
Critical speed zone	臨界轉速範圍		

第三章　輪機文書

（Writing Marine Engineering）

　　儘管輪機屬高度技術性的工作，但文書工作的重要性，以及輪機人員在此所需投入的時間與力氣，卻有持續增加的趨勢。所幸，這些文書工作皆已有可依循的寫法與要領。因此，身為輪機員，只要願意及早熟悉這些「輪機文書」，便能隨著資歷和努力的累積而駕輕就熟，並可望「寫」出心得。

　　在本章當中，我們先從輪機日誌的登載開始，接著是船上必備證書和文件、意外事故報告、電子郵件及燃油文件。而本章最後，是找工作所不可或缺的個人履歷。

第一節　輪機日誌登載（Engine Room Log Book Entry）

　　翻開輪機日誌，首先會看到對本輪船體、主機、發電機組、鍋爐等基本描述及輪機部門人員的職稱與姓名。

一、日常與特殊登載事項

1. 日期、航次、目的港

   Date and voyage where the ship is heading

2. 船位

   The position of the ship (at sea, at port or at anchorage)

3. 主機運轉參數

Readings and parameters of main propulsion engine

4. 發電機（輔引擎）運轉參數

Readings and parameters of auxiliary engine (generators)

5. 其他機器運轉參數

Readings and parameters of other running machineries

6. 主機轉速及設定負荷

Main engine RPM and load on the engine

7. 航速

Speed of the ship in knots

8. 各種潤滑油存量

Daily Entry for all the lube oil rest or remaining onboard

9. 各種燃料存量

Daily entry for all grade of fuel oil remaining onboard

10. 油渣與艙底水殘留量

Remaining onboard quantity of sludge and bilge

11. 重要機器運轉時數

Running hour counter for important machinery

12. 防止油污染設備運轉詳情

Details of oil pollution prevention equipment (e.g. time, position)

13. 重要故障及理由

Record of any major breakdown and reason

14. 機艙中事故

Record of incident or accident in the engine room

15. 船事故

Record of grounding, collision and other accidents

16. 重要機器翻修

Record of major overhauling of important machineries

17. 所有燃料的添加

Record of all bunkering operation (time, place, quantity)

18. 油渣與垃圾之處置

Record of all sludge and garbage disposal operation

19. 當值期間完成之其他工作

Remarks for additional work done in a watch

20. 船舶檢驗及PSC檢查

Remarks for surveys and port sate control (PSC) inspection

二、主機之登載

1. 當值時段

   Timing of watch (1200~1600; 1600~2000; 2000~0000)

2. 油門桿設定

   Fuel lever settings (notches)

3. 轉速設定

   Speed setting

4. 主機負荷

   Engine load

5. 轉數

   Engine revolution counter

6. 平均轉速

   Average rpm

7. 燃油表讀數

   Flow meter reading

8. 主機四小時油耗

   Main engine fuel consumption for 4 hours

9. 主機各缸排氣溫度

   Main engine all units exhaust temperature

10. 活塞水及缸套水溫度

Piston cooling water and jacket cooling water temperature

11. 主機燃油入口溫度

Main engine fuel oil inlet temperature

12. 冷卻器海水入口與出口溫度

Coolers sea water inlet/outlet temperature

三、冷凍空調單元（RAC Units）

1. 冷媒壓力

Suction pressure and discharge pressure of refrigerant

2. 滑油壓力

Lube oil suction and discharge pressure

3. 空氣溫度

Air inlet and outlet temperature

四、冰庫溫度（Compartment Temperatures）

1. Meat room

2. Fish room

3. Vegetable room

4. Dairy room

5. Handling room

五、淡水製造機 （Fresh Water Generator）

1. 缸套水溫度

Jacket cooling water in & out temperature

2. 冷凝器海水溫度

Condenser sea water in & out temperature

3. 殼溫

Shell temperature

4. 真空度

Vacuum

5. 噴射泵壓力

Ejector pump pressure

6. 蒸餾水泵壓力

Distillate pump pressure

7. 給水壓力

Feed line pressure

8. 水表讀數

Flow meter reading for fresh water

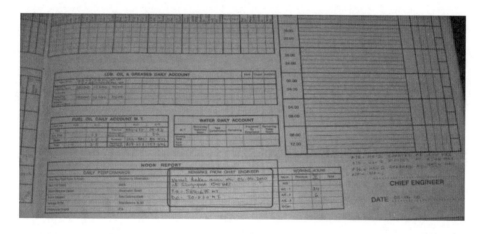

以下是輪機日誌登載必須注意的事情，請讀者反覆朗讀，並試著和實務聯想在一起。

As a part of engine room watch keeping routine, Marine engineers are required to keep a log of all important machinery parameters such as pressures and temperatures in the engine room log book.

This daily record-keeping book is a complete log of engine room readings which are compared with the design and trial conditions at regular intervals of time to analyze the performance of engine room machinery and systems. Additionally, the log book parameters are also checked during surveys and investigations related to any kind of incident in the engine room.

When this is the case, the log book's appearance is unavoidably affected, and as a result, alternatives and corrections should be reduced to a minimum. And the best way to avoid corrections is careful planning in advance.

以上這三段有關輪機日誌登載的說明告訴我們：

1. 當值輪機員須記錄所有主要機器的溫度與壓力等重要運轉參數。
2. 這些紀錄，平時可用來與設計值相較，以了解機器和系統的運轉狀況。此外，為了船舶檢驗或一旦遇到狀況，這些數據也將用於佐證。
3. 登錄在輪機日誌上的東西是具備法律效力的，不能用橡皮擦擦掉或以立可白蓋掉。若有寫錯，應直接劃掉、修改，並請輪機長在旁邊簽名。
4. 為盡量避免這類失誤，最好在登載之前先打草稿做好準備。

一、輪機日誌登載的幾個要領

（一）預留足夠時間來記錄參數

Duty Engineers often take rounds at the very end of the watch, carrying out the process in haste, overlooking some important machinery and missing several important parameters. About one hour before the watch gets over, the Duty Engineer should take a thorough round of the engine room, noting downall important parameters.

（二）在穩定狀態下記錄數據

To prevent that the data is useless and inevitably reflects changes in the condition or capability of crucial engine components, it is always advisable to take the readings when the engine room and all machinery systems are in steady conditions.

（三）記下重要事情、意外事故、故障及有驚無險的事情

Any unusual changes in the function of any machinery, sudden increase or decrease of parameters, accidents, near misses, or breakdown of any equipment should be entered and highlighted in the log book. Any important event taking place in the engine room should also be noted in the log book.

（四）記下槽、櫃的正確液位及相關輸送細節

Fill out important tank level figures. In case it is required to carry out transfers between any tanks, the same should be noted down in the log book with the final parameters. In case the transfer process is going onwhen watch is over, inform about the same to the incoming engineer and note the levels of the tanks at the end of your watch in the log book.

（五）常保輪機日誌整潔

The data in the log book are extremely important records which should be properly visible for future references. So, engineers must ensure that the log book is kept neat and clean. It is strongly suggested to use a proper cover for protection to prevent the log book from getting torn or spoilt.

（六）只用原子筆，並須在更正部分旁邊簽字

Use only ballpoint pen to fill the log book. If wrong readings have been written by mistake, they should be crossedout and correct readings must be written beside them.

輪機英文

（七）僅限值輪機員登載輪機日誌

It is the duty of the watchkeeping engineers to fill out and sign the log book at the end of every watch.

二、其他需要考慮的事項

（一）有關空氣污染防制證書

For marine engines with an Engine International Air Pollution Prevention (EIAPP) Certificate that are subject to the Engine Parameter CheckMethod as part of periodical IAPP Surveys, all changes to an engine's NO_x influencing components, including like-for-like replacements, are to be documented space in the Record Book of Engine Parameters.

（二）輪機日誌的其他用途

It is to note that a log book is not just for filling records but also to be used as a reference to study previous data of machinery parameters and to compare them with the current data, for understanding the condition of machinery systems and early detection of any major fault.

接下來我們就主機（柴油引擎）備便及添加燃油與潤滑油，列出一些經常用來登載在輪機日誌當中的例句。

一、主機備便（Stand-by Engine）

例如本輪主機（Main Engine, M/E）於13:05備便（S/B），離開漢堡。這時，要記下主機轉數及燃油錶上的數字。14:40 本輪完全出港、停止動俥，放大洋（Full away, F/A）。這時，我們將燃油（Fuel Oil, F.O.）溫度，逐漸調高到攝氏85度。到了15:10（在30分鐘內）將A油（Marine Diesel Oil, MDO）換成C油（Heavy Fuel Oil, HFO）來使用，再次記錄燃油錶讀數，隨即將主機轉速提高到在最大連續額定值（Maximum Continuous Rating, MCR）。

1. Departure from Hamburg. S/B 13:05, M/E counter meter 01345678. F.O. meter 0259612, F/A 14:40. F.O. temp. gradually raised to 85℃.

2. A oil changed to C oil in service *within 30 min*. F.O. meter 0259620. M/E speed raised to MCR.

3. F.O. temp, lowered to 85℃ within 30 min. C oil changed to A oil in service 07:00. F.O. meter 0259700.

4. *Arrived in Antewerp for anchorage*. S/B 08:20, Counter meter 01345900. *F.W.E.* 10:00. Counter meter 01346200. F.O. meter 259801.

5. S/B 08:00. F.W.E. 09:00. Arrival at *Port Said* for anchorage.

6. S/B 13:06. F.W.E. 15:00. *Moored alongside No.2 Pier.*

7. *Passing English Channel*. Engine stand-by.

8. Passing *Gibraltar Strait*. Engine stand-by.

9. Passing *Suez Canal*. Engine S/B all day. Passing *Panama Canal*, engine S/B all day. Passing *Singapore Strait*. S/B 06:00, F/A 07:00.

10. *Obtained W/H permission to carry out M/E T/C water washing*. S/B 08:00 T/C R.P.M. 3000 maintained. Average exhaust temp. 200℃.

After finishing washing, W/H noticed. Dead slow ahead 09:05. Slow ahead 09:15. Half ahead 09:45, F/A 10:05.

11. *Fire-extinguishing & life boat drills*, S/B 10:00, 10:05. Half ahead 10:10. F/A 11:00.

12. *M/E warming up* started19:00.

13. Cooling fresh water of M/E warm-up started to 50℃ 19:00. No.1 F.W. cooling pump started 06:00.

14. *Turning gear of M/E engaged* and started 08:00.

15. Compressed air charged into the air reservoir up to 30 kg/cm².

16. Turning gear of M/E disengaged. *M/E air purged* and fuel-running tried.

17. *W/H to C/R telegraph* tested and found in good condition.

18. No.1 G/E started 08:00, and put in parallel running.

19. F.O. temp. raised (or lowered) to 85℃ 10:00. A oil changed to C oil (or C to A oil) in service 09:00. Aux. blower of M/E stopped.

20. R.P.M. of M/E increased step by step, and fuel handle set to M.C.R. position.

21. M/E fuel temp. changed from 100℃ to 110℃ *on account of different fuel viscosity*.

22. No. 1 fuel oil purifier started 07:00. L.O. purifier started 09:00.

23. Aux. blower of M/E started 13:30.

24. M/E turned for 30 min. by turning gear, then stopped.

25. Main lubricating oil pump stopped.

26. Main F.W. cooling pump stopped, *after cyl. temp. dropped*.

27. M/E speed increased to 120 RPM 12:00.

28. M/E speed decreased to 115 RPM 24:00.

句號	英文	意思
2	within 30 min.	在30分鐘內
4	Arrived in Antewerp for anchorage	抵達安特衛普（比利時）下錨
4	F.W.E.	結束用俥（Finished with engine）
5	Port Said (Egypt)	賽得港（埃及）
6	Moored alongside No.2 Pier.	移泊二號碼頭
7	Passing English Channel	通過英吉利海峽
8	Gibraltar Strait.	直布羅陀海峽
9	Suez Canal, Panama Canal, Singapore Strait	蘇伊士運河、巴拿馬運河、新加坡海峽
10	Obtained W/H permission to carry out M/E T/C water washing	駕駛台（Wheelhouse）准予進行水洗主機過給氣機（Turbocharger）
11	Fire-extinguishing & life boat drills	滅火及救生艇演練
12	M/E warming up	主機暖機
14	Turning gear of M/E engaged	轉俥機接上
16	M/E air purged	以空氣清潔主機、吹缸
17	W/H to C/R telegraph	駕駛台通控制室俥鐘
21	On account of different fuel viscosity	基於燃油黏度的考量
26	after cyl. temp. dropped.	在氣缸溫度下降之後

二、添加燃油與潤滑油（Bunkering & LO Filling）

1. 08:00 to 16:35. *Fuel MDO 95.17MT, MFO 800.13MT* received at Yokohama. *Pumping commenced at 08:55* and finished at 16:00.
2. Cylinder oil 5000 liters received *in bulk* 09:00.
3. *M/E LO* 6000 liters received in bulk 09:30.
4. *G/E LO* 2000 liters received in bulk 10:00.
5. Turbine oil 200 liters received *in drum*.
6. Refrigerator oil 54 liters received in can.
7. Hydraulic fluid oil 400 liters received in drum.

8. Kerosene 400 liters received in drum.

9. Kerosene 200 liters transferred from deck to engine room daily tank.

10. Cylinder oil pumped from storage tank to daily measuring tank with hand pump 08:00.

11. *FO shifted from No.2P to No.2S double bottom tank due to inclining of ship* 13:05-14:10.

12. Nos. 3 & 4, P & S double bottom tanks filled with *fuel oil additive*, (Mixing ratio 1/2000).

13. Fuel oil mixed with sea water in No.4S tank. F.O. transfer pump discharge valve *flange dismantled*. Sea water pumped out.

14. LO 600 liters drained from storage tank into G/E sump tank.

15. All LO of M/E sump tank transferred to settling tank, heated up to 85℃, then poured back into M/E sump tank after 48 hours.

16. Camshaft LO tank of M/E cleaned. *LO 1100 liters renewed*.

句號	英文	意思
1	Fuel MDO 95.17MT, MFO 800.13MT	船用柴油（Marine diesel oil）、船用燃料油（Marine fuel oil）
1	Pumping commenced at 08:55	開始泵送油
2	in bulk	散裝
3	M/E LO	主機滑油（Maine engine lubricating oil）
4	G/E LO	發電機滑油（Generator engine lubricating oil）
5	in drum	2200公升桶裝
6	in can	罐裝
11	FO shifted from No.2P to No.2S double bottom tank due to inclining of ship	由於船傾斜，燃油從2號左舷雙重底櫃送到右舷
12	Fuel oil additive	燃油添加劑
13	Flange dismantled	拆下法蘭盤
16	LO renewed	換新滑油

第二節　船上必備的證書和文件（Certificates & Documents）

一、所有船舶皆須備妥的文件

1. 國際噸位證書
   International tonnage certificate
2. 國際載重線證書
   International load line certificate
3. 國際載重線豁免證書
   International load line exemption certificate
4. 完整穩定性手冊
   Intact stability booklet
5. 損害管制計畫與手冊
   Damage control plans and booklets
6. 最低安全配員證書
   Minimum safe manning document
7. 滅火安全訓練手冊
   Fire safety training manual
8. 火災控制計畫
   Fire control plan/booklet
9. 船上訓練與演習紀錄
   On board training and drills record
10. 防火安全操作手冊
    Fire safety operational booklet
11. 船長、甲級船員或乙級船員證書
    Certificates for Masters, officers or ratings
12. 國際防止油污染證書
    International oil pollution prevention certificate

13. 油料紀錄簿

Oil record book

14. 船上油污染緊急應變計畫

Shipboard oil pollution emergency plan

15. 國際防止污水污染證書

International sewage pollution prevention certificate

16. 垃圾管理計畫

Garbage management plan

17. 垃圾紀錄簿

Garbage record book

18. 航行數據紀錄系統——遵循證書

Voyage data recorder system—certificate of compliance

19. 貨物繫牢手冊

Cargo securing manual

20. 遵循證明

Document of compliance

21. 安全管理證書

Safety management certificate

22. 國際船舶保全證書

International ship security certificate (ISSC)

23. 連續概要紀錄

Continuous synopsis record (CSR)

二、貨輪（除上述證書之外，貨輪尚須具備以下文件）

1. 貨輪建造安全證書

Cargo ship safety construction certificate

2. 貨輪安全設備證書

Cargo ship safety equipment certificate

3. 貨輪安全無線電證書

  Cargo ship safety radio certificate

4. 貨輪安全證書

  Cargo ship safety certificate

5. 豁免證書

  Exemption certificate

6. 載運穀物授權證書

  Document of authorization for the carriage of grain

7. 油污染損害民事責任相關之保險或其他金融安全證書

  Certificate of insurance or other financial security in respect of civil liability for oil pollution damage

8. 加強檢驗報告書

  Enhanced survey report file

9. 最後壓載航行之油排放監控系統紀錄

  Record of oil discharge monitoring and control system for the last ballast voyage

10. 貨物信息

  Cargo information

11. 散裝輪手冊

  Bulk carrier booklet

12. 專用清潔壓載艙操作手冊

  Dedicated clean ballast tank operation manual

13. 原油洗艙操作與設備手冊

  Crude oil washing operation and equipment manual (COW manual)

14. 狀況評估計畫

  Condition assessment scheme (CAS)

15. 遵循聲明

  Statement of compliance, CAS

16. 最終報告與審查紀錄

CAS final report and review record

17. 靜水力平衡裝載操作手冊

Hydrostatically balanced loading (HBL) operational manual

18. 油排放監控操作手冊

Oil discharge monitoring and control (ODMC) operational manual

19. 隔艙與穩定信息

Subdivision and stability information

三、客輪（除一般船舶證書之外，客輪尚須具備以下文件）

1. 客輪安全證書

Passenger ship safety certificate

2. 豁免證明

Exemption certificate

3. 特種業務客輪安全證書、特種業務客輪艙間證書

Special trade passenger ship safety certificate, special trade passenger ship space certificate

4. 搜尋與救援合作計畫

Search and rescue co-operation plan

5. 運轉限制清單

List of operational limitations

四、在某特殊船舶上還可能須備妥以下證書

1. 化學船：裝載散裝危險化學品適切證書（Certificate of fitness for the carriage of dangerous chemicals in bulk）、危險貨物清單或配載計畫（Dangerous goods manifest or stowage plan）

2. 氣體運送船：裝載散裝液態氣體適切證書（Certificate of fitness for the carriage of liquefied gases in bulk）

3. 高速船：高速船安全證明（High-speed craft safety certificate）、

高速船操作許可（Permit to operate high-speed craft）

4. 裝載INF貨物之船：載運INF貨物適切性國際證書（International certificate of fitness for the carriage of INF cargo）

5. 核子貨船：核子貨物安全證書或核子客船安全證書取代或船安全證書或客船安全證書（Nuclear cargo ship safety certificate or nuclear passenger ship safety certificate, in place of the cargo ship safety certificate or passenger ship safety certificate, as appropriate）

6. 特殊用途船：特殊用途船安全證書（Special purpose ship safety certificate）

7. 海域支援船：海域支援船適切性證書（Certificate of fitness for off-shore support vessels）

8. 潛水系統：潛水系統安全證書（Diving system safety certificate）

9. 動態支撐艇：動態支撐艇建造與設備證書（Dynamically supported craft construction and equipment certificate）

10. 移動式海域鑽採裝置：移動式海域鑽採裝置安全證書（Mobile off-shore drilling unit safety certificate）

11. 翼地效應艇：翼地效應艇安全證書（Wing-in-ground craft safety certificate）、翼地效應艇操作許可（Permit to operate WIG craft）

12. 噪音程度：噪音檢驗報告（Noise survey report）

第三節　事故報告（Accident Reporting）

　　一篇事故報告所呈現出的樣子，對於看報告的人會如何看待此一事故和接下來將採取的作為，影響甚鉅。其格式益顯重要，事故當中最重要的事情，必須在第一段和第二段當中闡明。為確保受到重視，我們應將所發生的事情，盡量精簡扼要、摘要敘述，舉例如下：

At 0130 hrs on the 10th October, 2016, whilst on passage from Suez to Aden, a fire was discovered in the engine room chemical store. The alarm was raised and the crew went to fire stations and carried out the appropriate fire fighting operations and successfully extinguished the fire at 0155 hrs. Passage to Aden was resumed at 0210 hrs, and the ship arrived at Aden on the 12th October where minor fire damage repair was carried out. No injury was sustained by the personnel on board and the members of the emergency team who fought the fire are to be congratulated for how they respond to the accident.

以上段落在於簡短的告訴公司忙碌的經理：

1. The ship has a fire;
2. Says where the fire was;
3. The incident was quickly dealt with and passage was resumed with the minimum delay;
4. There were no injuries to personnel;
5. The response and training were very good.

針對此事件的檢討，主要在於如何將這類事故再次發生的可能性減至最低。因此，我們接著在報告當中，可以這麼建議，希望得到好的收尾。

As a result of this incident it is recommended that the following actions be taken:

1. Instructions be issued as a matter of urgency informing the Fleet that chemicals, oils and greases, and waste, must not be stored in the same store room;
2. Instructions be issued to the effect that quantities of calcium hypochlorite should be kept to a minimum and kept in a steel container;
3. Advices be circulated to all crew members as to the correct fire extinguishing medium to be used in dealing with chemical fires.

以下是幾個不同類型事故報告的實例：

一、斷電事故

To: Port Engineer, Taipei

Date: October 11, 2016

From : Engine Department, M.V. LinChuen

Subject: Report on Electric Failure

During maneuvering at departure from Long Beach, a blackout took place, due to an electric failure of No. 1 generator. It caused short circuit at main switchboard and tripped the other paralleled generator subsequently.

This generator was inspected. It revealed that the whole stator (exciting coil) twisted for about 120 degrees. The wire connection of excitation part broke off consequently and caused short circuit, due to excessive exciting current.

An adequate repair was carried out. The generator is ready for use. To prevent the same problem from happening again, I decided to fix the stator by welding a beam to it. And a small hole was made on port side for further inspection.

Thank you for your kind attention. Your understanding in the matter will be much appreciated.

Chan Yonan

Yon-An Chan

Chief Engineer, M.V. LinChuen

二、艉軸管油封漏油

October 31, 2016
To: Port Engineer
From: Chief Engineer, M.V. Tainan Victory

Subject: Starboard Stern Tube Oil Seal Leakage

Voyage: 31W/E

After leaving the Suez Canal on the westward leg of the subject voyage, No.1-2 seal of the starboard stern gland was found leaky, and 120 liters/day of oil was lost from the head tank although there had been no leakage prior to arrival. On the European Coast it was found that there was no leakage from the seal whilst the engine was turning slowly or stopped even with the head tank valves open. This was verified carefully for several hours in various ports.

After leaving Europe, a test was carried out with an attempt to reduce the loss of oil by isolating the head tank and increasing the stern tube bearing oil pressure. But this resulted in a heavy influx of water into No.1-2 and also No.2-3 seal. As this might have resulted in water getting into the stern tube bearing, the head tank for No.1-2 seal was again brought into operation. At present, the oil loss is still in the region of 120 liters/day. There was also a slight leakage of water to No.2-3 seal. This water was drained off periodically. However, in the Suez and in Port Kelang & Singapore on the westward leg there was still no leakage of oil outward when the engine was stopped with the head tank valves open.

The oil tank for No.1-2 seal on top of the engine room gives a head of 0.3M above sea level when the ship is loaded to the maximum draft of 12.3M. However, our draft is normally about 11.5M giving a head above-sea level of 0.8M and sometimes more when traveling between local ports. At present, the seal oil head is increased by means of a temporary tank. But I recommend that modifications be carried out on both port & starboard sides. The oil level head is adjusted between 10.0 and 12.5M.

Chan Chang, Tu
C. C. Tu
Chief Engineer
M.V. Tainan Victory

三、處女航報告

May 18, 2016
To: Engineering Department
From: S.B. Sha
Chief Engineer
M.S. ChinMing

Subject: Maiden Voyage Report, Engine Department

The M.S. ChinMing was handed over at 11:00, May 18, 2016. The vessel proceeded to anchorage at 11:42. During the three days at Yokohama, we completed all final work, and received bunkers and lubricating oil. The engine room staff familiarized themselves with all the pipelines and machinery equipments.

The vessel sailed at 13:00, May 19. During the 10 days after sailing, we found that M/E sump tank sounding pipe reading gradually dropped. It revealed that the lubricating oil of M/E was lost. After 10 days of searching, we found that the pipe flange of one lubricating oil line wasn't tightened up. It was under the site of M/E. The tightening work was neglected by the dockyard. I requested the guarantee engineer to prove the situation, and asked for compensation. About 2000 liters of lubricating oil was lost before the leakage site was found. The flange bolts were tightened by ship's hand.

At 16:00, May 29, M/E was stopped for inspection after running for 15 hours, 1000 liters of new lubricating oil were loaded into the sump tank. All lubricating oil filters were removed, dismantled, cleaned and restored. All F.O. filters were cleaned throughly. The sea chest strainers were opened up and cleaned.

At 20:00, May 30 the engine was re-started. After 6 hours running, the engine stopped at 04:00, May 31. No. 2 cylinder fuel valve cooling water did not flow in the inspection tank. The pipes were dismantled section by section, and found the metallic pellet jammed inside the pipe. The pipes were cut, obstruction removed, and then joined by rubber hose temporarily.

The emergency fire pump didn't have good pressure. We had tried everything since departure but nothing availed. The guarantee engineer said that the ship was in ballast condition, the fire pump was too high out of the water, and should be designed to have a sufficient suction in any loaded condition.

The alarm system of the F.O. purifier was not quite good. No alarm would sound when the purifier was out of order. We were checking the pressure switch.

After the ship had left Yokohama, the engine speed was maintained at 114 RPM for one day, and then reduced to 100 RPM. It consumed 75 tons of fuel per day, during the sea trial. The heating steam to the fuel oil wing tank was closed. It was enough to operate the turbo-generator only. But the weather got colder day by day and the steam to all wing tanks were opened, so we could not maintain the steam pressure with exhaust gas economizer. The aux. boiler ignited. The steam inlet valve to steam coil was closed 1/3 turn. The steam was not enough to warm the heavy fuel oil. The fuel oil transfer pump always tripped due to high viscosity.

The speed of the M/E increased to 111 RPM. It helped the steam pressure a lot, but the fuel consumption increased to 97 tons/day. To save the fuel, we adjusted the steam to fuel oil wing tank. The M/E speed was reduced to 101 RPM and its diesel generator was paralleled with the turbo-generator. There was still no sufficient steam. So the M/E speed was adjusted to 102.5, and the rate of consumption was 79 tons/day. The steam to all fuel tanks was partly opened. The fuel was warm enough without tripping the transfer pump. The fuel consumption of the diesel generator (half load) was 2.5 tons/day. The lubricating oil daily consumption was 76 liters. The rate was nearly normal. The cylinder oil consumption was 700-840 liters/day according engine's RPM. The rate was 1.3 g/BHP/Hr. It was reduced to 1.2 g/BHP/Hr (640 liters/day) according to maker's instruction book.

The main & aux. engines' performance was in a very good condition throughout the voyage. The aux. boiler's burner starter contactor was burned out, due to frequent cut-in or cut-out. The burner assembly was removed for overhauling. The gangway lights were found without source, as they were not connceted to the distribution box. No water tight switches were installed according to the drawing.

輪機英文

No major problems have been encountered, and all minor defects have been overcome. The engine department personnel have worked very hard to maintain a good maiden voyage and succeeded.

Wang, Shia

Wang, Shia
Chief Engineer
M.S. ChinMing

四、主機五號氣缸蓋

May 20, 2015
To: Port Engineer
From: M.B. Lin
Chief Engineer
M.S. May Ming

Subject: Number 5 Cylinder Cover

This is to submit the following report about the subject cylinder cover leakage mentioned in our telex to you dated May 18, 2015.

While turning main engine by turning gear at Hamburg on the 15th of May the water leakage was seen from No.5 unit cylinder cover indicator valve. The unit was dismantled and the cylinder head was tested after having blanked the cooling water inlet passage of the cylinder cover guide ring. During the hydraulic test under gravity water was found leaking from the visible cylinder cover facing corresponding chamber and between indicator valve & air starting valve pocket as shown in the sketch. In all previous cases of cylinder cover failures, the cracks have developed from within the recess for air starting valve and indicator valve of cylinder cover due to corrosions caused mainly by low cooling water temperature.

In compliance with maker's recommendations for minimizing corrosion in and around area the main engine and piston cooling water temperatures have been raised to 78℃ and 67℃ respectively since the 17th of May, 2015. Furthermore, all cylinder covers of the main engine have got inserted insulation tubes following:

1. Has the crack developed due to the maintenance of higher jacket area cylinder cooling water temperature?

2. Have the inserted insulation tubes in cooling bores caused the interference with uniform cooling of the bored area around the insulation tubes?

3. Have the inserted insulation tubes caused the turbulence in cooling water-flow giving rise to non-symmetrical cooling of the area in and around insulation tubes?

We suggest this cylinder cover failure should be made known to the engine maker for review and their comments, if any, in order to avoid this kind of trouble. We'd also request you to arrange for repairing the defective cylinder cover on this vessel's arrival at a port where it is convenient to do so.

Shin Tnag Tseng
S.T. Tseng
Chief Engineer, M.V. MayMing

五、發電機燃油錶故障

Date: July 8. 2017

To: Port Engineer

From: Sun Lin

Chief Engineer

M.S. Pin Rong

Subject: Failure of generator diesel oil flowmeter

On June 28, 2017 at 0600 hours, a fuel oil flowmeter failure occurred which caused a black-out for a few seconds, while the vessel was approaching Hong Kong.

No.1 & No.3 diesel generators had been running in parallel with a share load of 370 kW each. The low frequency alarm sounded in the control room. Both the generators tripped and the S/B No.2 generator was started, but it could not run up to full speed. A black-out in the E/R, caused the M/E shut-down. Meanwhile the first engineer on duty, found a blockage in the fuel line to the generators. The diesel oil flowmeter by-passed immediately, allowed the diesel oil to flow freely into the engines, "preferential and emergency" had functioned smoothly. No.3 generator was able to sustain the remaining load and electrical power was re-established within a few seconds. All tripped pumps were started, and the main engine was re-started again. The ship's navigation maintained. No.1 generator engine could not be re-started immediately. Its fuel oil system had become "air locked" due to blockage of diesel oil. It took about half hour to prime all the filters, fuel pumps and injectors, before they could be run up to full speed and put on load.

When the situation became normal, the cause of the sudden black-out was investigated. The filter before the diesel oil flowmeter was found very clean. The flowmeter was then dismantled. It was found that the gear assembly and rotor were clogged heavily with oil sludge. All parts were cleaned with kerosene. However, the gear assembly was found misaligned already, and the gears loosened on the fine bearings. Hence it could not turn freely. This was the cause of 'the jam of flowmeter, and consequently resulted diesel oil did not flow through to the engine. Diesel oil flowmeter was then by-passed, and diesel oil daily consumption was estimated by sounding. Please refer to the ship's requisition form No. 10346, dated May 12 and supply a diesel oil flowmeter as soon as possible, I wish to mention once again that the continuous use (over 3 months) of diesel oil with high sulfur content has caused these severe consequences. Please refer to my letter dated. The use of dirty diesel oil has not only caused the flowmeter's malfunction, but also the loss of power for the ship to mobilize, during the navigation in a busy sea passage. Hence it is very essential to supply diesel oil free of sludge to the ship at Hong Kong.

What is said above is for your information and necessary action. Thank you for your kind attention.

Truly yours

Jinchen Chen

J.C. Chen
Chief Engineer, M.V. PinRong

第四節　電子郵件（Email Writing）

　　寫 Email 是當今各行業在國際間最常見的聯繫方法，以下舉一些在各種場合配合各類需要可能用上的 Email 實例，作為參考。

一、學生因缺課寫給老師

From: Jack Hu

Sent: Monday, March 01, 2016 8:02 PM

To: Jian Hua

Subject: Monday's class

Dear Dr. Hua

　　I would come and see you in person but I know you were not in office this afternoon, so I thought I should still write to you about this. I am so sorry for missing Marine Engineering English class this morning. I really have no excuse. Somehow my alarm did not go off and I honestly did not wake up until the end of the period. This is not an excuse and I understand it perfectly that this is not acceptable at all. All I have to say is it was never my intention to miss the class. I will try to come see you tomorrow and make sure I know what I have to prepare for the next class meeting, if that's fine with you.

Thank you,

Jack

二、要求在線上重交報告

Dear Jian,

　　I am very sorry to bother you again. Some kind of errors occurred during the compiling of the report form, anyway we cannot access it. Could you please complete the report form again and submit it via the system?

Thank you very much for your help and your time. If you need any further assistance or for any questions and/or problems, please do not hesitate to contact me.

Best regards,

Lucia

三、寫給工作同仁、安排參訪、同仁回覆

Folks,

You have previously expressed an interest in visiting Walter Redfield's power station. I've set up this date for a visit. I figure it will take about 1/2 hour travel time each way and about a 1 hour visit, so we should finish up just before noon. Email me for willingness to join us.

Brian

（同仁回覆）

Hi Brian,

Thanks for the invite. I am definitely interested and wonder if it would be the sort of thing we should and could bring friends along, or should we wait until the end of semester? Let me know when.

Thanks again.

Donnie

四、謝謝同仁寄照片來

Jian,

I just now ran into this email and had not opened the pictures. Thanks for taking time to take them and send them to me.

Paul

Looks great to me, Jian. Many thanks.

Terry

五、邀請同仁同行、完成任務

David,

I switched our project to Thursday morning, 8/10. Jian & I should be there about 8:00 a.m. I anticipate it taking no longer than 2 hours to drop and disassemble the tower.

Raphael, would you like to help out?

Brian

Folks,

Here's what we wanted to be doing here at this point in time if we had not had all the obstacles put in front of us with our program.

Paul

Folks,

Facilities can't cut loose of the truck for tomorrow, so the expedition to Norris is off. I do have the truck reserved for next Thursday, though. I'm looking into a car for tomorrow for the Sustainability Fair in Butte.

Brian

Folks,

　Sorry for the last minute announcement but: anyone interested please attend!

Harry Sheski

Folks,

　Here is an opportunity for your consideration.

Harry Sheski

第五節　船用燃料相關文件（Documentation for Marine Bunker）

　船上所用的燃料不僅關係到船的正常運轉與營運成本，也直接影響輪機人員在使用這些燃料的過程中，所可能面對的各種問題。為確保添加到船上的燃料在數量和品質上皆符合船上所需，船上輪機部門有必要確實了解燃料相關文件內容，並視需要提出恰當的交涉。以下分別就燃料供應合約、油料紀錄簿、燃油分析報告、加油收據、抗議或申討信，說明其用途和主要內容。

一、供應合約（Bunker Supply Contracts）

　The supply of bunkers is agreed between the supplier and the ship operator on a separate contract to the charter party. The ship operator will enter into contractual relations with the bunker supplier usually based on the supplier's standard terms. Caution is to be exercised in accepting standard terms during negotiations of bunker supply contracts as they are usually particularly onerous on the purchaser.

Bunker Details EXAMPLE

| Bunker Ref. No | BDN Ref. No. | Port Date | Supplier Name | Fuel bunkered Specs (BDN) | | | Bunkered In | | C/E sign |
			Barge/Truck /Installation	Grade	Density at 15°C (kg/m³)	Sulphur (% m/m)	Tank no.	Quantity (MT)	
Example 01/09	12345	Pusan 02.01.09	Korean Man Korea 1	RMG 35	0.9782	3.5	2 (P) 2 (S)	250 400	
Example 02/09	34567	Pusan 02.01.09	Korean Man Korea 1	RMG 35	0.8422	0.9	1 (P)	130	

BDN: BUNKER DELIVERY NOTE
Note: The Bunker Ref. No. should be in serial order starting from the month of January i.e. serial No. /year (e.g. 01/09)

The company safety management system must include instructions and procedures for bunkering. Chief Engineer should post the bunkering instructions at the bunker station for all parties involved to read. Good bunkering practice should ensure that these instructions are read and fully understood before any bunkering commences.

BIMCO Standard Bunker Contract
CONFIRMATION NOTE
Sellers and Buyers hereby confirm the bunker nomination as follows:

1. Place of Nomination	2. Date of Nomination
3. Sellers (Cl. 1)	4. Buyers (Cl. 1)
5. Vessel	6. Port or Place of Delivery/ETA (Cl. 5)
7. Product(s)/Specifications (Cl. 2)	
8. Grade(s)/Quantities (Cl. 2 and Cl. 3)	
9. Price(s)/Currency (Cl. 7)	
10. Delivery Means and Additional Charges (Cl. 7)	
11. Payment (Cl. 8)	
12. Min. Hourly Pumping Rate (Cl. 9(c)(ii))	13. Compensation Rates for Delay (Cl. 9(c))
14. Dispute Resolution Alternative Agreed (Cl. 15)	
15. Additional Clauses, if any	

Approved by
The International Bunker
Industry Association

Copyright, published by
The Baltic and International Maritime Council (BIMCO), Copenhagen
Issued: November 2001

All terms and conditions of the "BIMCO Standard Bunker Contract", which the Buyers have had the opportunity to familiarise themselves with, and any agreed amendments thereto, including the Dispute Resolution Clause, are herewith incorporated and shall apply to the delivery of Marine Fuels contracted for above.

二、油料紀錄簿（Oil Record Book）

總噸數（Gross tonnage, GT）大於150的油輪和大於400以上的非油輪，都須在船上備妥油料紀錄簿（Oil record book, ORB）Part I，以記錄機艙中的有關運轉事項。此外，150 GT以上的油輪還須備妥ORB Part II，以記錄貨油與壓載的操作。這些紀錄在於用作該船遵循防止污染法規的佐證。請讀者反覆朗讀以下相關規定，並聯想其在實務上的意思。

1. It is one of the most important documents onboard with a written record for compliance of MARPOL Annex I.

2. When operating oily water separator (OWS), 15 ppm equipment for discharging treated bilge water overboard, the operation is recorded with time, position of ship, quantity discharged and retention.

3. Maintenance operation of MARPOL equipment e.g. OWS, sewage treatment plant and incinerator should be recorded with the type of maintenance, date and time.

4. Any internal bilge or sludge transfer to be recorded with date and time and quantity transferred.

5. Any maintenance on OWS is recorded and acknowledged by engineering officer carrying out the operation.

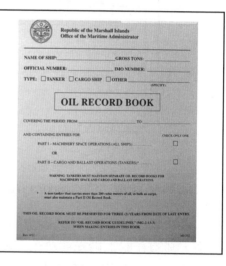

以下所列為油料紀錄簿登載的注意事項，請讀者反覆朗讀，並試著聯想相關的實務工作。

1. The Oil Record Book Part I shall be readily available for inspection. It shall be preserved for a period of three years after the last entry has been made.

2. When making entries in the Oil Record Book Part I, the date, operational code and item number shall be inserted and the required particulars shall be recorded.

3. Each completed operation shall be signed and dated by the officer or officers in charge. The Master of the ship shall sign each completed page.

4. In the event of accidental or other exceptional discharge of oil, statement shall be made in the Oil Record Book Part I of the circumstances of, and the reasons for, the discharge.

5. Any failure of the oil filtering equipment shall be noted in the Oil Record Book Part I.

6. Weekly retention of waste water that includes bilge and sludge system to be recorded.

7. It should always be accompanied with International Oil Pollution Prevention (IOPP) certificates and all the receipts of bunker and sludge/bilge disposal operation.

8. All the operation and records are acknowledged by officer carrying the job along with Chief Engineer signature.

9. At the end of every page, Master will sign the oil record book.

10. Bunkering operation to be recorded including date, time, bunkering grade, quantity bunkered, port of bunkering, and retention of used in bunkered operation.

以下為美國國土安全局和海岸巡防署所提供的ORB格式範例：

FORM APPROVED
OMB No. 1625-0009

**U.S. Department of
Homeland Security**

**United States
Coast Guard**

OIL RECORD BOOK
FOR SHIPS

CHECK ONE: ☐ This book is for Machinery Space Operations (Part I-All Ships)

☐ This book is for Cargo/Ballast Operations (Part II - Oil Tankers)

Name of Ship: ☐   Official Number: ☐

Owner: ☐   Gross Tonnage: ☐

Period From: ☐   To: ☐

**THIS BOOK MUST BE MAINTAINED ABOARD THE SHIP FOR AT LEAST THREE YEARS
FOLLOWING THE "TO" DATE LISTED ABOVE.**

As per 33 Code of Federal Regulations (CFR) 151.25, this record book is issued by the Secretary of Homeland
Security and is distributed by the United States Coast Guard to ships of American registry. It remains the property of
the United States Government and each owner/operator is responsible to maintain and surrender it in accordance
with the Secretary's regulations. Note that the Oil Record Book is *one* book with two parts; Machinery Space
Operations is under Part I and Cargo/Ballast Operations is under Part II.

Each oil tanker of 150 gross tons and above, ship of 400 gross tons and above other than an oil tanker, and
manned fixed or floating drilling rig or other platform shall maintain an Oil Record Book Part I (Machinery Space
Operations). An oil tanker of 150 gross tons and above or a non oil tanker that carries 200 cubic meters or more
of oil in bulk, shall also maintain an Oil Record Book Part II (Cargo/Ballast Operations).

Oil Record Books printed by the U.S. Government are available to the masters or operators of all U.S. ships
subject to 33 CFR 151.25, from any Coast Guard Sector Office, Marine Inspection Office, or Captain of the Port
Office.

An agency may not conduct or sponsor, and a person is not required to respond to a collection of information unless it displays a valid OMB control
number. The Coast Guard estimates that the average burden for each response is 2.5 minutes. You may submit any comments concerning the
accuracy of this burden estimate or any suggestions for reducing the burden to: Commandant (CG-CVC-1), U.S. Coast Guard, 2100 2nd Street SW
Stop 7581, Washington, DC 20593-7581 or Office of Management and Budget, Paperwork Reduction Project (1625-0009), Washington, DC 20503.

Clear guidance should be given to ship's personnel on how to complete correctly the ORB. It is suggested that a standard format for entries is adopted by the owner's ships to try to avoid the possibility of fines from Port State Control (PSC) or others for incorrect record keeping. All entries in the ORB must be in ink. Writing in pencil in any log record should be avoided, and all entries should be made at the time of the operation to avoid mistakes.

The entries in the ORB should be considered accordingly. The areas of most concern are the entries required when:

- related to oil residue (sludge and other residues) retained onboard the ship,
- transferring or disposing of oil residues,
- operating the oily water separator, when non-automatic disposal methods are used,
- transferring and collecting bilge water to the bilge tanks and any oil residue (sludge) content of the bilges,
- related to other operations required, that is removal of any bilge or oily water separator piping or valves for maintenance purposes

The Chief Engineer is responsible for ensuring that the ORB is correctly maintained. The Master should regularly check the ORB to see that it is correct. This important document, if not accurately completed, can lead to the ship's Master and/or Chief Engineer being fined or detained. It should be noted that all entries in the ORB must be wholly true and accurate. Fines for falsifying ORB entries can be greater than $2m and result in imprisonment.

三、燃油分析報告（Fuel Oil Analysis Reports）

歸納起來，一套完整且準確的燃油分析報告可為船上帶來以下好處。請讀者反覆熟讀，並試著配合如下分析報告實例與輪機實務聯想在一起。

1. Confirmation that bunkers as received meet purchase specifications

(or do not meet specs, as the case may be),

2. provides warning of contaminant levels, incompatibility, excessive water content, etc.,

3. enables engineers to adopt suitable strategies for proper utilization of the fuel,

4. provides permanent independent third-party report (analysis) of fuel oil received and enables owner to claim against bunker supplier in case of failure to meet purchase specifications or in case of delivery of unmarketable product,

5. shoreside laboratory will normally alert owner to any unusual or potentially damaging characteristics or fuel oil and will suggest countermeasure strategies.

Oiltest Marine Services - Marine Fuels Analysis Report

- Vessel Name   M/V BANCHIO
- Port Bunkered   BEAUMONT
- Date Bunkered   2/22/2008
- Suppliers Name   BUNKER FUEL
- Grade   MSC DMA (MOD)

	Result	Specification
Density, kg/m3 @ 15C	874.5	890.0 Max
Viscosity cSt @ 40C:	2.6	1.5 6.0 Min / Max
Flash Point, Deg C	69.4	6 0.0 Min
Pour Point, Deg C	-24	0 Max
Sulfur, %m/m	0.2	1.00 Max
Cetane Number:	40.6	40
MCR, % m/m	0	0.30 Max
Ash, % m/m	0.00	0.010 Max
Total Sed, Exis., % m/m:	0.00	Max
Water, % v/v	0.00	Max
Vanadium, mg/kg	0	
Sodium, mg/kg	0	
Silicon, mg/kg	0	
Aluminum, mg/kg	0	
Appearance:		CLEAR and BRIGHT

This sample analysis has met and is within all of the Marine Fuel specifications for the grade as stated.

The single most important constraint in this process is time. It is highly desirable to have the results of the shoreside fuel oil analysis available to the owner (and, of course, the ship's engineer) before the fuel is to be used and the damage done. Normal practice requires that new bunkers are segregated from existing bunkers to the greatest extent possible.

四、加油收據（Bunker Receipts）

MARPOL公約Annex VI 當中第18條規定，所有船上添加的燃油都須提供收據（Bunker delivery receipt）。此收據須留存在船上三年，準備隨時接受檢查。以下為相關須知和表格實例，請熟讀之。

The bunker delivery receipt is to be signed by the Bunker Barge Master and the Chief Engineer or Master of the ship receiving fuel oil. The Chief Engineer should sign only documentation stating "for volume at observed temperature only" as there can be no certainty of any weight figures for the fuel loaded. If fuel oil is taken in a country that has not ratified MARPOL Annex VI, the supplier is not required to issue a bunker delivery receipt that complies with MARPOL requirements. However, the ship may require suitable documentation to satisfy port state control officers at subsequent ports.

IBIA Standard Bunker Delivery Note/Receipt

IBIA Standard Bunker Delivery Note / Receipt

© 2006

Supplier Details

Nomination No.	
Company Name	
Address 1	
Address 2	
Address 3	
Address 4	
Telephone	

Date	
Port	

Company Name	
Vessel Name	
IMO Number	
Flag	
Shore Tank	
Bunker Barge	
Pipeline	
Road Tank Wagon	

Product Details

Grade/ISO Designation	
Density @ 15°C (kg/m³)	
Calculated from Components	YES / NO
Shore Tank measurement	YES / NO
Bunker Tanker measurement	YES / NO
Viscosity (mm²/s) @ 50°C	
Flash Point (°C)	
Sulphur % (m/m)	
Water Content % (m/m)	

	Opening Gauges					Closing Gauges				
Tank No.	Tank Gauge (corrected for trim)	Observed Volume in litres	Observed Temperature	Volume Correction Factor	Standard Volume @15°C	Tank Gauge (corrected for trim)	Observed Volume in litres	Observed Temperature	Volume Correction Factor	Standard Volume @15°C
1										
2										
3										
4										
5										
6										
7										
8										

Total Standard Volume (A) / Total Standard Volume (B)

Total Volume transferred = A-B
Standard Volume @ 15°C (m³) (A-B)/1000

Event Log									
ALONGSIDE		CONNECTED		START PUMPING		FINISH PUMPING		DISCONNECTED	
Date	Time	Date	Time	Date	Time	Date	Time	Date	Time

Density @ 15°C (kg/m³)
Delivered MASS Tonnes (kg/1000) in vacuo
Weight Correction Factor
Delivered MASS Tonnes (kg/1000) in air

	Receiving Vessel	Bunker Tanker	MARPOL	Surveyor
Seal Numbers				

Remarks	I, the undersigned declare that the fuel oil supplied is in conformity with regulation 14(1) or (4)(a) and regulation 18(1) of MARPOL Annex VI	Stamp of vessel/signature of vessel officer
	signed	
	Name (Print)	

輪機英文

Bunker Delivery Note

MARPOL SPECIFICATION FORM

SHIP NAME	SHIP IMO NUMBER
BUNKER PORT	BUNKER DATE
SUPPLIER NAME	SUPPLIER ADDRESS
DATE OF COMMENCEMENT OF DELIVERY	BARGE NAME

BUNKER INFO FUEL GRADE:		SULPHUR:	% m/m
QUANTITY:	MTons	DENSITY:	kg/m³ @ 15°C

This is to certify that the fuel oil supplied conforms to MARPOL regulations.

_____   _____
Signature of Chief Engineer   Signature of Supplier Representative

五、抗議或申討信

　　一旦針對添加燃油的數量出現爭議，船長必須盡快發出一封申討信（Letter of protest）。信中至少要涵蓋以下幾點：

1. 日期與時間

    Date and time fuel oil was loaded

2. 船名

    Name of ship receiving the fuel oil

3. 短少數量

    Volume shortage

4. 添加油等級

    Grade of fuel oil loaded (or thought to have been loaded)

5. 短少百分比

    Percentage shortage in relation to the order

6. 供油廠商

    Name of bunker supplier

7. 供油船名

Name of bunker barge or shore facility

8. 收據號碼

Bunker delivery receipt reference number

此信由船長和／或輪機長簽名，並遞送副本。

The letter of protest should be signed by the Master and/or the Chief Engineer. It should be directed to the barge Master or shore representative and copied to the following interested parties:

- shipowner or manager
- charterer (if time charter fuel oil)
- organization or laboratory analyzing the fuel oil
- bunker supplier
- bunker broker

如可能，這封申討信最好也能讓加油船的船長或岸上代表簽名，並蓋上本輪和該油船的正式戳印。以下為這類信件的實例。

```
Date_____
Ref_____
To _____ (Master Cargo Officer of Barge etc)
   _____ (Address)
   _____ (Address)

Dear Sirs:

LETTER OF PROTEST FOR BUNKERING OPERATION ON _____ (date)

I, Chief Engineer of M/V _____ (name of vessel)
Short received _____ tones of _____ (grade of bunkers)
Out of the _____ tones requested for on _____ (date bunkers received).
The bunkers were supplied by barge/tanker/shore tank _____ (name)
Ref No. _____ on _____ (date) at _____ (location).
I hereby lodge a protest against short delivery.
Yours faithfully


_____
(name of Chief Engineer)
cc:                     Ship Owner/Manager, fuel analysis Service
Duplicate copy to:      Fuel Supplier


                    ACKNOWLEDGED RECEIPT
_____
Signature of Master/Cargo Officer of Bunker Barge/Tanker/Shore Tank


_____    _____
Name of Master/ Cargo Officer of Bunker Barge/Tanker/Shore Tank      Date & Time
```

第六節　輪機員的履歷（Resume for Marine Engineer）

　　在一位輪機專業人員的工作生涯當中，往往會不只一次，需要「找工作」。而英文履歷（Resume），往往是這份工作所徵人才的基本要求。值得注意的是，個人履歷書信正是和徵才公司的首次接觸。其重要性不言可喻。請先反覆閱讀以下段落，並試著和自己找工作這件事，聯想在一起。

Resume is a personal advertisement of professional related skills and job experience. It has to be good enough to get the desired result and should be simple and target oriented. These resume example is a technique to build an effective and successful resume. The goal of the resume is to help employers in picking your profile from thousands of job applicants. These resume makes use of proper jargon that meets the industry standards. These examples will help you in achieving a job interview.

所以，如何在尚未能和未來雇主見面之前，藉著這份履歷讓他們認識你，並留下好印象，便成了在眾多競爭者當中脫穎而出，所不可或缺的關鍵。國際間徵求輪機專業人才的廣告範例如下：

Technical Manager

We are looking for a Technical Manager who would be responsible for day to day operations of the vessels, carry out regular inspections, dry-dockings of the vessels to ensure compliance with regulations. Other duties will include budgeting, financial reporting and other managerial responsibilities.

Candidate requirement:

- Seafaring experience
- Minimum of 3 years as Chief Engineer on Offshore Support Vessels
- Maritime Degree or equivalent
- Over 5 years' of relevant shore based experience in the offshore industry
- Strong communication skills across different corporate levels
- Demonstrated leadership and management in multinational environment

Our Client offers competitive package and opportunity to work in diverse multicultural environment. Priority will be given to candidates who live and work in Singapore.

一、輪機員履歷開場信（Cover letter）樣本

儘管徵才廣告上無此要求，請記得，在準備你的履歷的同時，一定要寫一封簡單的Cover letter作為開場，和履歷一道寄出。以下是這封信的範本。

DaLin Chen
1958 ShinFeng Street
Keelung, Taiwan 20221
0958-147-148
dlchen@gmai.com

Apr 24, 2017

Ms. Karen Gao
Fingiang Marine Group
4271 Ninbo W. Road
Taichuen, Taiwan 40078

Dear Ms. Gao,

I am applying for the Marine Engineer position now available with Fingiang Marine Group.

I have a bachelor's degree in Marine Engineering and my studies centered on hydrodynamics, calculus, physics, chemistry and mechanical engineering. I also took courses in hydrofoils, offshore structures and hydrostatics. To gain a better understanding of this position and everything it entails, I completed an internship where I worked side by side with professional engineers.

I gained experience in the construction of boats and ships of all sizes and I have extensive knowledge of the steering, propulsion and other vessel systems. I have the knowledge and training needed to oversee test that help to determine if the systems are functioning correctly and to make sure they comply with all rules, regulations and standards. When there is a problem, I have the skills to make repairs to all systems, equipment and structures to make corrections where needed.

I have the ability to analyze data, modify and upgrade engine designs along with the equipment used on the engines and the vessels. I can provide estimates for new projects or for repair jobs and I have the ability to keep excellent records of all work performed.

I have excellent problem solving and time management skills, lots of patience and the ability to work and make good decisions independently. My skills and training matches the requirements in your posting and I hope to meet with you soon to discuss the details of this position.

You can reach me for an interview by calling 0958-147-148

Respectfully,

Your Signature
DaLin Chen
Enclosure: Resume

[Your Name]
[Street Address]
[City, St Zip]
[Optional – Email Address]

[Today's Date]

[Name of Recipient]
[Title]
[Company]
[Address]
[City, St Zip]

Dear [Name of Recipient],

[Introduce yourself and what job you would like to be considered for. Try to personalize the introduction if possible by including details about past encounters with the recipient or details about third parties who may be referring you to the job. Make it interesting so the reader will continue reading. See the Cover Letter Template page for more tips.]

[Discuss 3 or 4 characteristics or traits that set you apart. Provide stories, facts and details which demonstrate these traits in the work place. Consider using formatting such as bullets, bold and italics to draw attention to important information.]

[Close by wrapping it all up and calling the reader to action. Ask them for an interview or a response]

Sincerely (or Respectfully Yours),

[Sign here for letters sent by mail or fax]

[Typed Name]

Enclosure

輪機英文

以下是幾份輪機員履歷範本：

AnSuen Chin

78-1Alley 6, Lane 75, Nanking E. Road Sec. 3

Taipei, Taiwan 10512

0953-789-123 aschin@yahoo.com

Objective:

To be able to work as a Marine Engineer in a first class international vessel where I can impart my skills and knowledge in Marine Engineering areas such as survival techniques, handling marine equipment of up to 12750kW, maneuvering engineering systems and other related machineries. These skills will help the company achieve its mission of providing a safe voyage to its passengers and crews.

Education:

- National Taiwan Ocean University, MS in Marine Engineering, 2003.
- National Kaohsiung Maine University, BS Marine Engineering, 1999.

Skills:

- Engineering Training Course Level III.
- Knowledgeable in survival techniques and safety responsibilities.
- Oil Spill Response Training.
- Ability to operate repulsion machinery of 750 K.W.
- Strong familiarization of engineering systems such as propulsion systems, bilge and fire systems, and HVAC systems.
- Working knowledge on fuel injectors, fuel pumps, steams, and other related machineries.

Professional Experience:

Chief, Marine Engineer, 2008-Present,
Kaohsiung Marine Company, Kaohsiung, Taiwan

Responsibilities:

- Operated and maintained propulsion systems and controls, bilge and fire systems, electrical components and HVAC systems.
- Evaluated equipments before installation to ensure that all parts are complete and none is missing.
- Managed the overall audits of the ships for local and international voyages.
- Ensured reliable and safe operations for every trip by providing safety and survival techniques to crews.

1st Assistant Engineer, 2005-2008,
Taiwan Marine Company, Taipei, Taiwan

Responsibilities:

- Supervised team for ship repair and dry-docking projects and oil spill response.
- Supervised maintenance of fuel injectors, fuel pumps, steams, and other related machineries.
- Trained a team of Marine Engineers on the operation of power plants and steam generation before deployment.
- Participated in the planning and preparation of cargo activities for a more efficient operation.

2nd Assistant Engineer, 2003-2005, M.V. Star Bright

Responsibilities:

- Operated and maintained propulsion systems and controls, bilge and

輪機英文

fire systems, electrical components and HVAC systems.

- Evaluated equipments before installation to ensure that all parts are complete and none is missing.

- Managed the overall audits of the ships for local and international voyages.

- Ensured reliable and safe operations for every trip by providing safety and survival techniques to crews.

1st Assistant Engineer, 2005-2008,

Florida Marine Company, Miami, FL

Certifications and Affiliations:

- Certificate in Proficiency in Survival Crafts and Rescue Boats.
- Association of Certified Marine Engineers of Wales.
- Competency as Marine Engineer 1st Class.

An Der Lin

6 FL 782 Ninan Street

Keelung, Taiwan 20223

0953-789-123

adlin@gmail.com

Summary:

A versatile, accomplished engineering professional with proven years of expertise managing marine operations in a wide range of industrial settings; Exhibits a strong and firm approach to sustaining and encouraging safe work environments, and a demonstrated ability to streamline operations; Strong skills in directing and motivating staff; Fluent in the English language; Possess a wide range of technical expertise on various aspect of marine operations; Articulate and highly organized individual.

Professional Experience

Senior Marine Engineer January 2007 – present
VIC, Shanghai, China

Responsibilities:

- Designed, operated, maintained and repaired mechanical systems of ships.
- Inspected machinery and equipment and made sure that the equipment works properly before the ship is launched.
- Specialized in repair and maintenance of ship when it is in dry dock.
- Accounted for equipment installations on ships.
- Trained crew to operate the ship's equipment at sea.

Junior Marine Engineer June 2004– January 2007
CSC, Gulfport, MS

Responsibilities:

- Designed and oversaw testing, installation, and repair of marine apparatus and equipment.
- Worked on various studies such as analytical, environmental, operational, or performance studies in order to develop designs.

Marine Engineering Staff February 1999 – May 2004
Green Life Engineering, Qingdao, China

Responsibilities:

- Designed, operated, maintained and repaired mechanical systems of ships.
- Inspected machinery and equipment and made sure that the equip-

153

ment works properly before the ship is launched.

- Specialized in repair and maintenance of ship when it is in dry dock.
- Accounted for equipment installations on ships.
- Trained crew to operate the ship's equipment at sea.

Junior Marine Engineer June 2004– January 2007

CSC, Gulfport, MS

Education:

Master of Science in Engineering, Kaohsiung Technological University, Taiwan Bachelor of Science in Ocean Engineering, National Taiwan Ocean University, Taiwan.

Skills:

- Excellent command of the English language.
- Organization skills.
- Written and verbal communication.
- Interpersonal skills.
- Relationship building.
- Innovative approach.

Awards and Honors:

Society of Naval Architects and Marine Engineers, Member Marine Engineers Beneficial Association, Member.

Mei Sing Lo

78-1Alley 6, Lane 75, Fuchien Road

Gaosiung, Taiwan 80013

0953-789-123

mslo@yahoo.com

Job Objective

Looking for work as Marine Engineer in which to develop and enhance my training and experience in this field.

Highlights of Qualifications

- Hands-on experience working as a Marine Engineer.
- Deep knowledge of Marine Management.
- Exceptional knowledge of naval architecture.
- Immense ability to work offshore.
- Ability to interpret schematics and engineering specific drawings.
- Outstanding skills in constructing marine boats.
- Skilled to perform failure analysis on equipment.
- Capable to manage multiple projects.

PROFESSIONAL EXPERIENCE

Marine Engineer, August 2005 – Present
Shing Hwa Steel Corporation, Kaohsiung, Taiwan

- Designed and tested all marine equipments and associated apparatus.
- Developed designs for marine engines, structures and equipments and conducted analysis on same.
- Prepared drawings, layout and necessary schematics of marine equipments on ship.
- Analyzed data and ensured that it could be manufactured, resolved

輪機英文

all issues in same and made necessary modifications in design.

- Conducted various environmental and performance tests on machinery and equipment and ensured they were in compliance with company's standard.
- Maintained marine equipments and machinery, inspected and completed all job requests for same.
- Coordinated with shore and ship's captain and ensured that schedule and budget of ship were maintained.
- Ensured that all design, estimates and schedules created were in accordance to international regulations.

Marine Engineer, May 2000 – July 2005
Bechtel, Singapore

- Managed contract managements and hob estimate for marine.
- Manufactured and produced medium sized steel and aluminum boats.
- Prepared schedule of project and procured all raw materials.
- Filed all documents for control systems.
- Coordinated with customer relations team and solved all problems.

Education:

Bachelor's Degree in Marine Engineering, Ocean University of China, Qingdao, China.

二、信封格式

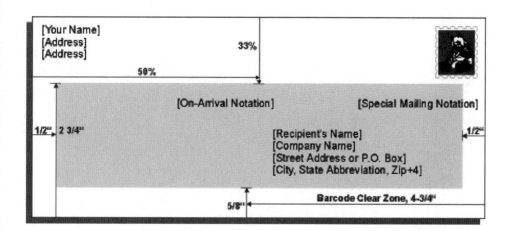

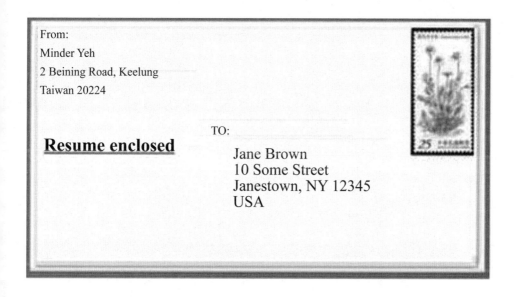

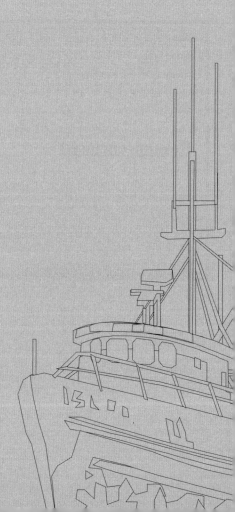

第四章 測驗例題

I. Choose the best word for the blank:

(A) 1. Don't you have any question _____ [A. about   B. above   C. but   D. below] turbocharger?

(C) 2. _____ [A. At   B. Above   C. For   D. From] what interval shall we have to wash the blower side?

(A) 3. You'll have to wash the air filter once _____ [A. every   B. nearly   C. over   D. below] month.

(D) 4. The sponge filter called "Everlight Scott" is fitted _____ [A. in   B. above   C. below   D. around] the air filer.

(A) 5. This pipe is _____ [A. where   B. when   C. within   D. about] you will fit the water washing tube and hopper.

(B) 6. What _____ [A. give   B. does   C. go   D. is] the water washing mean?

(A) 7. Pour several cups of fresh water _____ [A. from   B. around   C. below   D. underneath] here, the water is induced into the blower.

(A) 8. Dusts sticking _____ [A. upon   B. above   C. below   D. about] the impeller wheel are taken off by the striking force of water droplet.

(C) 9. _____ [A. Where   B. When   C. How   D. About] is the engine speed at the washing time?

(A) 10. It is all right to keep the engine speed as it _____ [A. is   B. use   C. go   D. can].

(A) 11. How _____ [A. about   B. above   C. but   D. can] the engine speed when we wash the turbine side?

(C)　12. The engine speed must be slowed down _____ [A. from　B. around　C. below　D. underneath] that of 50% load.

(B)　13. I agree _____ [A. in　B. with　C. by　D. on] you, Chief.

(C)　14. This testing room seems to be equipped _____ [A. in　B. above　C. with　D. of] everything necessary for the tests.

(B)　15. All necessary chemicals are on the shelf _____ [A. in　B. at　C. within　D. with] the right side.

(B)　16. Cocks fitted _____ [A. in　B. above　C. between　D. onto] the left side basin are for taking boiler water samples.

(A)　17. For water analysis, all readings are to be plotted _____ [A. against　B. across　C. into　D. of] the design theoretical line.

(D)　18. It's quite a different form _____ [A. within　B. above　C. by　D. from] what we had in my former ship.

(D)　19. Count _____ [A. in　B. above　C. by　D. on] me, you'll soon get used to it.

(A)　20. All information is returned _____ [A. to　B. above　C. between　D. off] the Chief Engineer after completion.

(B)　21. That's _____ [A. within　B. about　C. below　D. off] the same practice as I followed before.

(B)　22. The supply for auxiliaries may be derived _____ [A. in　B. from　C. by　D. of] the main sea-water system too.

(B)　23. It's a little bit low. Pump them up _____ [A. in　B. to　C. by　D. of]their maximum pressure.

(A)　24. Next step is to put _____ [A. in　B. above　C. by　D. of] the engine turning gear.

(D)　25. Are the cylinder mechanical lubricators full _____ [A. in

B. above   C. by   D. of] oil?

(C) 26. Check that they work correctly _____ [A. in   B. above   C. by   D. of]hand.

(C) 27. A turbo-blower is rotated _____ [A. in   B. above   C. by   D. of] the exhaust gases leaving the engine.

(B) 28. Heating coils in bunker tanks are necessary _____ [A. in   B. for   C. by   D. of]heating.

(B) 29. Some poor-quality marine fuel oil start to solidify _____[A. in   B. at   C. by   D. of]normal temperatures.

(D) 30. The marine fuel cannot be re-liquefied by heating _____ [A. in   B. above   C. by   D. under]this circumstance.

(A) 31. This pipe is where you fit _____ [A. in   B. above   C. by   D. of]the water washing tube and hopper.

(B) 32. It is all right to keep the engine speed _____ [A. in   B. as   C. by   D. of] it is.

(C) 33. In that case, the engine speed must be slowed down _____ [A. in   B. above   C. below   D. of]that of 50% load.

(C) 34. The induced water may be vaporized _____ [A. within   B. above   C. unless   D. under] the temperature of turbine side is lowered.

(C) 35. The temperature of turbine side is lowered _____ [A. in   B. above   C. by   D. of]reducing the engine speed.

(A) 36. _____ [A. Give   B. Use   C. Go   D. Run] the engine a turn.

(B) 37. Pay attention _____[A. for   B. to   C. afloat   D. into] maintaining the correct temperature of the fuel oil.

(B) 38. The first job is to start up the circulating pump to warm _____ [A. around   B. up   C. going   D. about] the main engine.

(A) 39. Start No. 3 generator and put it _____ [A. in   B. above   C.

161

by   D. of] parallel operation with No. 2 generators.

(C) 40. Cooling water for the M.E. is circulated _____ [A. for   B. above   C. by   D. of] a centrifugal pump.

(C) 41. The watering will be finished _____ [A. of   B. into   C. in   D. at] about fifteen minutes.

(A) 42. The cylinder oil is flowing _____ [A. at   B. with   C. about   D. between] all the sight glasses.

(C) 43. Can you take less_____ [A. on   B. under   C. in   D. around] price?

(D) 44. The boiler's function is to generate steam_____ [A. around   B. under   C. out   D. from] water.

(B) 45. Open the warming steam valve slightly to inject steam _____ [A. of   B. into   C. in   D. around] the water system.

(C) 46. How many tons can be supplied _____ [A. of   B. into   C. in   D. around] an hour?

(A) 47. Which pump shall we use _____ [A. for   B. above   C. by   D. of] this cruise, No.1 or No.2?

(C) 48. How can I set the pump _____ [A. of   B. into   C. in   D. around] such a condition?

(C) 49. The water can reach around 55℃ _____ [A. for   B. above   C. by   D. of] the time of the engine trial.

(C) 50. Shall I stop the turning to take _____ [A. around   B. under   C. out   D. from] the turning gear?

(D) 51. All lubricating oil sumps are filled _____ [A. as   B. around   C. of   D. to] the correct level.

(B) 52. How_____[A. old   B. often   C. big   D. long] do pistons need to be withdrawn usually?

(A) 53. Dusts sticking upon the blades are taken _____ [A. off   B.

above   C. around   D. about] by the striking force of water droplet.

(A)   54. Test the air drain cock _____ [A. for   B. through   C. to   D. over] water and impurity.

(B)   55. Oil holes drilled in the cylinder liner must go _____ [A. for   B. through   C. to   D. over]. (B)

(A)   56. If you want to increase the amount of oil supply, set the lever _____ [A. at   B. into   C. above   D. through] lower side.

(C)   57. _____ [A. Into   B. At   C. For   D. With] what interval shall we have to wash the blower side?

(A)   58. This pipe is where you will _____ [A fit   B. keep   C. make   D. operate] the water washing tube and hopper.

(A)   59. What _____ [A. does   B. make   C. is   D. below] the water washing mean?

(A)   60. If you pour several cups of fresh water from here, the water will be induced _____ [A. into   B. at   C. for   D. with] the blower.

(B)   61. It is all right to _____ [A. fit   B. keep   C. make   D. operate] the engine speed as it is.

(D)   62. In that case, the engine speed must be slowed down _____ [A. does   B. make   C. is   D. below] that of 50% load.

(A)   63. Release part of water discharging to sea back to the pump suction can _____ [A. adjust   B. drive   C. remove D. close] sea water temperature.

(B)   64. It's time to start preparations _____ [A. on   B. for   C. into   D. with] sea.

(A)   65. This is really my first experience _____ [A. in   B. over   C. of   D. above] this ship.

163

輪機英文

(A) 66. You can do your job with me as far _____ [A. as   B. above C. over   D. on] today is concerned.

(C) 67. I'll give you help and advice if necessary and your questions are always _____ [A. refused   B. favored   C. welcome   D. concerned].

(A) 68. Well, how can I _____ [A. set   B. do   C. drive   D. control] the pump in such a condition?

(A) 69. I'll try to get rid _____ [A. of   B. on   C. with   D. at] all air in the system by means of the air cocks.

(A) 70. Open the warming steam valve slightly to inject steam _____ [A. into   B. on   C. off   D. above] the water system.

(A) 71. If the oil has been undisturbed in the drain tank for a long period, a sample should be _____ [A. drawn   B. driven   C. put   D. removed] from the bottom.

(B) 72. Pass [A. after   B. through   C. with   D. below] the critical speed zone quickly although the revolutions must be reduced gradually.

(A) 73. Pay close attention to the water temperature and try to [A. adjust   B. drive   C. drew   D. remove] the valve if the temperature tends to fall.

(A) 74. Three generators are operating [A. in   B. on   C. with   D. at] parallel.

(A) 75. From the outlet of the fresh water distiller the water is led [A. back   B. above   C. over   D. onto] to the suction of the pump.

(C) 76. The control valve is governed [A. at   B. above   C. by   D. of] engine inlet temperature.

(A) 77. A oil changed to C oil _____ [A. in   B. into   C. for   D.

at] service 15:10. F.O. meter 0259620.

(C) 78. Arrived in Antewerp _____ [A. in B. into C. for D. at] anchorage.

(B) 79. Compressed air charged _____ [A. in B. into C. for D. at] into the air reservoir up to 30 kg/cm^2.

(A) 80. W/H to C/R telegraph tested and found _____ [A. in B. into C. for D. at] good condition.

(A) 81. No.1 G/E started 08:00, and put _____ [A. in B. into C. for D. at] parallel running.

(D) 82. R.P.M. of M/E increased step by step, and fuel handle set _____ [A. in B. into C. for D. to] M.C.R. position.

II. Fill blank with appropriate word

1. M/E speed raised to maximum continuous r_____ng.　　（rating）

2. The boiler must consist of a f_____e in which fuel may be burned efficiently.　　（furnace）

3. The boiler must consist of a c_____n chamber in which fuel may be burned efficiently.　　（combustion）

4. The boiler must consist of a heat t_____r surfaces which allow the energy to reach water contained within the boiler and so to form steam.　　（transfer）

5. The boiler must consist of a chamber to allow steam and water to s_____e.　　（separate）

6. The boiler must consist of a d_____t which allow for the escape of flue gases to the atmosphere.　　（duct）

7. The boiler must consist of various f_____ngs which ensure that the supplies of fuel, air, and feed water are balanced with the demand for steam.　　（fittings）

8. The boiler must consist of various f_____ngs concerned with the safe operation of the boiler. （fittings）

9. The usual arrangement for motorships has sea-water c_____ion of coolers for lubricating oil. （circulation）

10. I know that it is one of important pr_____res before running the main engine. （procedures）

11. I have already re_____shed the oil. （replenished）

12. Make sure that all indicator valves are open and the man_____ring handle is in the stop position. （maneuvering）

13. A t_____ger is driven by a gas turbine, which is rotated by the exhaust gases leaving the engine. （turbocharger）

14. Heating coils in bunker tanks are necessary to make the fuel p_____able. （pumpable）

15. Some marine fuel oil have a p_____r point sufficiently high that they start to solidify at normal temperatures. （pour）

16. Because of low con_____ty the fuel cannot be re-liquefied by heating. （conductivity）

17. The boiler consists of various fittings concerned with the safe operation of the boiler, e.g. s_____y valve. （safety）

18. L_____ting oil is flowing uniformly from all the bearings. （Lubricating）

19. I have already confirmed the fresh water e_____n tank is full. （expansion）

20. The induced water is vaporized because of the high temperature of t_____e side. （turbine）

21. In salty water the soap can not d_____e like this. （dissolve）

22. The ducts allows for the escape of f_____e gases to the atmosphere. （flue）

23. Turning g_____r disengaged and telegraph test finished.

（gear）

24. What is the present pressure of the starting air r_____irs?

（reservoirs）

25. First switch on the non-fuse-b_____r of the No. 1 pump starter and push the start button. （breaker）

26. The usual arrangement for motorships has been to have sea-water circulation of coolers for l_____ting oil. （lubricating）

27. Open suction and d_____y valves of both pumps, as we are going to set No. 2 pump in stand-by condition. （delivery）

28. Observe this s_____ce strictly, otherwise the No. 2 pump can't be set in the stand-by condition. （sequence）

29. The air cocks should be in the highest p_____n. （position）

30. Adjust the o_____ning of the valve so that the temperature can reach around 55℃. （opening）

31. All lubricating oil sumps are filled to the correct l_____l.

（level）

32. Delivery and suction p_____res of cooling water are quite normal.

（pressures）

33. The usual arrangement for motorships has been to have sea-water circulation of c_____lers for lubricating oil. （coolers）

34. The engine fuel oil system should now be p_____med.

（primed）

35. I tended all parts which require hand supply of oil or g_____e.

（grease）

36. The induced water may be v_____zed unless the temperature of turbine side is lowered. （vaporized）

37. The boiler's function is to generate s_____m from water.
（steam）

38. In f_____e or combustion chamber fuel may be burned efficiently.
（furnace）

39. The supplies of fuel, air, and f_____d water are balanced with the demand for steam. （feed）

40. One of main functions of the feed water system is to transfer condensed steam from the c_____r to the boiler. （condenser）

41. There are three basic methods to control hot fluid in heat e_____ger.
（exchanger）

42. The d_____l engine burns its fuel within the engine itself, transferring energy directly to the working fluid. （diesel）

43. The construction of the engine is devoted to converting energy into useful m_____l work. （mechanical）

44. The high-pressure, high-temperature air resulting from the combustion act on a p_____n, which rotates a crankshaft. （piston）

45. The air c_____ks are on the top of the cylinder covers. （cocks）

46. Heating c_____ls in bunker tanks and particularly in double bottom tanks have always been necessary for heating to make the fuel pumpable. （coils）

47. The supply for a_____ries may be derived from the main sea-water system also. （auxiliaries）

48. If you want to e_____d the washing interval of the blower side you must wash this sponge once a week. （extend）

49. As far as a_____ty of lubricating oil is concerned, improved additive technology has eliminated the need for very high TBN cylinder oil. （alkalinity）

50. We do not foresee a need for total b_____e number above 80 for

cylinder oil. （base）

51. Even if temperatures of piston r_____gs are constrained, thermal loading of lubricating oils will be greater. （rings）

52. The generators are equipped with so-called automatic s_____zing equipment. （synchronizing）

53. Increase the mass of air following the work c_____e of diesel engine allows more fuel to be efficiently burned in the cylinder.

（cycle）

54. The air may be supplied to the engine under pressure by one of two m_____ms. （mechanisms）

55. We've changed fuel oil and are just about to reduce the r_____ns.

（revolutions）

56. When reducing the engine revolutions, be careful of the c_____l speed zone. （critical）

57. Three generators are operating in p_____l. （parallel）

58. The stand-by air c_____r started to fill up the air bottles.

（compressor）

59. The fuel oil and cooling water temperatures are m_____ned by adjustment of the related valves. （maintained）

60. Cooling water for the main engine is circulated by a c_____al pump. （centrifugal）

61. At the outlet, the water is taken to the fresh water d_____r and the heat is used for evaporating sea water. （distiller）

62. We c_____ct all kinds of boiler water tests here. （conduct）

63. This testing room has all testing kits and c_____cals necessary for boiler water test. （chemicals）

64. A square wooden box on the r_____ck is what they called "universal tester". （rack）

65. All you have to do for s_____ling is simply turn these cocks, and then an already cooled down sample comes out from here.

（sampling）

66. I have never seen such a convenient sampling d_____ce before.

（device）

67. Let me show you these two kinds of r_____rd books to be kept for boiler water testing.　　　　　　　　　　　　　　（record）

68. The report s_____et attached is also to be completed daily after the test.　　　　　　　　　　　　　　　　　　　　　（sheet）

69. Remaining q_____es of all test chemicals and apparatus are checked every seven days and the results are filled in this book.

（quantities）

參考文獻（References）

Blakey, T.N. (1987) English for Maritime Studies, 2nd ed., Prentice-Hall International, London.

Boris Pritchard. A DATABANK OF MARITIME ENGLISH RESOURCES – AN INVITATION FOR CONTRIBUTIONS. Faculty of Maritime Studies, University of Rijeka Studentska.

Born-Leichleitner I. Ibid. GUIDANCE OF CONTINUOUS MACHINERY SURVEY (CMS) (Ver.3) January 2013.

Born-Leichleitner I. Words, Words, Words...Dealing with Vocabulary in ESP. Views, Vol. 1, No 2, 1992, p.68.

Cole, C., P. Trenkner and B. Pritchard. 2004. Maritime English Learning Material Database (MarEng) www.leonardodavinci.fi/projects/stat/jatkoon2004.html.

Cole, C., Trenkner, P. (2001). The Thematic Network on Maritime Education, Training and Mobility of Seafarers, Paper presented at the Eleventh IMLA Workshop on Maritime English (WOME 11), Varna Bulgaria. Cunningsworth, A. (2003) Choosing your Coursebook. The Teacher Development Series, Macmillan Publishers Ltd.

Dudley-Evans, T., St. John, M.J. 1998. Developments in ESP: A Multi-Disciplinary Approach. Cambridge: Cambridge University Press, 1998, pp. 82-83.

Fan Miaofu (1993) English Correspondence for International Shipping Business, (Shangai, China: Baijia Press).

Fischer, C, and Trenkner, P (1990) English in Search and Rescue. Rostock, Germany: Hochschule fur Seefahrt Warnemunde/ Wustrow.

Grice, T. 2009. English for Mariners A Two-Level Course Book Published by Arbeitsbereich Linguistik, wwu Münster LdV-Project lcctv.

Grice, T. 2009. English for Mariners Guidance Notes for Teachers. Published by Arbeitsbereich Linguistik, wwu Münster LdV-Project lcctv.

Hutchinson, T., Waters, A. English for Specific Purposes: A Learning-Centred Approach. Cambridge: Cambridge University Press, 1987, p.19.

IMLA-IMEC.com (International Maritime English Conference, an IMLA website for Maritime English – formerly WOME; previous web address: home.planet. nl/~kluijven).

IMO, International Shipping Federation. www.marad.dot.gov, www.fma.fi, etc.

IMO. 2010. Engine Log Book Supplement.

Kamil, M.L. (Eds.), Teaching and Learning Vocabulary; Bringing Research To Practice. Mahwah, New Jersey, London: Laurence Erlbaum Associates, Publishers, 2005, pp. 27-30.

Katarzyska, B, (1988) Notes on Ships, Ports and Cargo, (Gdansk, Poland: Wydawnictwo Morskie Gdansk).

Kluijven, P. C. van. 2003. The International Maritime English Language Programme, An English Course for students at Maritime Colleges and for on-board. Alk & Heijnen Publishers.

Logie, C., E. Vivers, A. Nisbet (1998) Marlins English for Seafarers, Study Pack 2, Marlins, Edinburgh.

McDonough & Shaw (1993) Materials and Methods in ELT Oxford Blackwell.

Nation. I.S.P. Learning Vocabulary in Another Language. Cambridge: Cambridge University Press, 2001, p12.

Nautical Institute, London: www.nautinst.org (well known among ME teachers for its downloadable MARS reports (Marine Accident Reporting Scheme).

Nisbet, A. & A. W. Kutz & C. Logie (1997) Marlins English for Seafarers, Study Pack 1, Marlins, Edinburgh.

Olga Romanova. 2017. The importance of multilingual professional awareness: peculiarities of teaching maritime vocabulary. Baltic International Academy, Riga, Latvia.

Perry, D., MacDonald, P. Word Knowledge and Vocabulary Instruction, International Conference on Engineering Education, 2001, p. 8B3-11. http://www.ineer.org/Events/ICEE2001/Proceedings/papers/201.pdf.

Petkova, V. & S. Toncheva (2000) Correspondence and communications in Shipping, Handbook, Izdalelska k'isha STENO, Varna.

Pritchard, B. (2000) "Maritime VHF Communications: Standards versus Practice", In: Proceedings of Workshop on Maritime English (WOME 2A), IMLA, Dalian Maritime University, Dalian, China, 44-54.

Pritchard, B. (2003) On some aspects of evaluating Maritime English materials – checklist Proce Maritime Academy: 139-152.

Spinčić A. Luzer J. (1999): English in Marine Engineering Communication, Adami , Rijeka.

The Common European Framework of Reference for Languages. Cambridge: Cambridge University. Press, 2003, pp. 24-29. http://www.coe.int/t/dg4/linguistic/Source/Framework_EN.pdf Accessed February 10, 2008.

The International Maritime Human Element Bulletin. Effective communication. The key to successful operations. Issue No. 14 May 2007.

Trenkner, P. (1997) 'The IMO Standard Marine Communication Phrases as adopted. IMO-MSC 68', paper presented at WOME 9, Malmo, June 1-4, 1997.

Trenkner, P., C. Cole (2003) Raising standards by getting the Maritime English instructor shipshape – are our profiles at sea? Proceedings of IMEC 15, St.Petersburg, 7-10 Oct. 2003, IMLA & Admiral Makarov State Maritime Academy: 5-14.

Trenkner, P., Hartung, R., Struschka, B. 2003. Standardised (IMO-SMCP) Safety-related Maritime Radio Communication in Dialogues (Tasks) - Aufgaben 1, Loesungen 2.

Uribe-Echevarria (1997) Technical English I for Marine Engineers.

Wang Qinchao (1992) Practical English Conversation for Mariners, (Dalian, China; Dalian Maritime University Press).

Websites created and maintained by individual Maritime English teachers (http://home. planet.nl/~kluijven; http://www.pfri.hr/~bopri).

Winbow, A. The Importance of Effective Communication, International Seminar on Maritime English. 2002, p. 4. http://www.imo.org/includes/blastDataOnly.asp/data_ id%3D18000/InternationalSeminar.pdf Accessed.

Zhang, Shaolin, (1993) Practical English for Marine Engineers, (Shangai, Shangai -Scientific Technology Press.

附錄

一、輪機縮寫與代號（Terms for Marine Engineering）

縮寫與代號對照表如下：

（未納入下表當中的縮寫，可查：

1. http://www.marineterms.com/terms-dictionary/abbreviations/all.html
2. http://www.termisti.refer.org/nauterm/dicten.htm
3. https://karatzas.mobi/semaphore/maritime-abbreviations-basil-m-karatzas/）

AB, A/B	Ablebody seaman, Seaman 1st class	幹練水手、一等水手
AC, A/C	Air conditioning	空調，冷氣
2/E	Second engineer	大管輪
3/E	Third engineer	二管輪
4/E	Fourth engineer	三管輪
AC	Alternative current	交流電
ACB	Automatic circuit breaker	自動斷路器
ACB	Air circuit breaker	空氣斷路器
ACU	Auxiliary control unit	輔助控制單元
APS	Arrival pilot station	抵達領港站
AG	Arabian gulf	阿拉伯灣
AGW	All going well	一切正常
AL	Alpha lubricator	氣缸油注油器
A/S	Alongside	靠泊
API	American Petroleum Institute	美國石油協會
AFFF	Aqueous film-forming foam	水性成膜泡沫
AVR	Automatic voltage regulator	自動電壓調節器

BA	Breathing apparatus	呼吸輔助器
BAF	Bunker adjustment factor, %	燃油調整因子
BB	Bulbous bow	球型艏
B/C	Bulk carrier	散裝輪
BDC	Bottom dead center	下死點
BDR	Bunker delivery receipt	加油收據
BM	Beam	橫樑
BF	Bunker fuel	海運／航空燃料
BHP	Brake horsepower	制動馬力
BOSUN	Boatswain	水手長
BOB	Bunker on board	船上燃油
BOG	Blow-out gas	溢散氣
BROB	Bunkers remaining on board	船上燃油存量
BP	Boiling point	沸點、氣化溫度
BT	Bow thruster	艏推進器、側向推進器
CA	Crank angle	曲拐角度
CAD	Cadet	實習生
CAN	Controller area network	控制器區域網路
C/E	Chief engineer	輪機長
CAS	Condition assessment scheme	狀況評估計畫
CBM	Condition base maintenance	基於狀態保養（視情保養）
CCAI	Calculated carbon aromaticity index	計算碳芳香指數
CCU	Cylinder control unit	氣缸控制單元
CFE	Constant frequency electrical	定頻電
CG	Coast guard	海岸防衛隊
CNG	Compressed natural gas	壓縮天然氣
CII	Calculated ignition index	計算點火指數
CO Pump	Control oil pump	控制油泵
CoCoS	Computer controlled surveillance	電腦控制監控系統
COW	Crude oil washing	原油洗艙

C/P	Charter party	租船合同
CAR	Corrective action request	要求改正
CBM	Cubic meters	立方公尺
CBFT, CFT	Cubic feet	立方英呎
CBT	Clean ballast tanks	乾淨壓載艙
CFC	Chlorofluorocarbon compounds	氟氯碳化物
CHENG, C/E	Chief Engineer	輪機長
CHOF, C/O	Chief Officer, Chief mate	大副
CM	Contingency manual	應變手冊
CO₂	Carbon dioxide	二氧化碳
CONS	Consumption	消耗量
CR	Control room	控制室
CRS	Common rail system	共軌系統
CRN	Crane	吊桿
CROB	Cargo remaining on board	船上尚存貨物
CSR	Continuous synopsis record	連續概要紀錄
CST	Centistoke	厘鐸（黏度）
CVS	Consecutive voyages	連續航次
DC	Direct current	直流電
DC book	Damage control book	損害管制簿，損管簿
DE	Diesel engine	柴油引擎，柴油機
DFE	Dual fuel engine	雙燃料引擎
DFS	Dual fuel ship	雙燃料船
DFV	Dual fuel vessel	雙燃料船
DM	Distillate marine	蒸餾海運燃油
DMG	Direct mounted generator	直接安裝發電機
DMG/CFE	Direct mounted generator / Constant frequency electrical	直接定位裝卡發電機 ／ 恆頻電
D&A	Drug & Alcohol	毒品與酒
DET	Detention	扣船

輪機英文

DEV	Deviation	偏離航線
DISCH	Discharge	排出（量）
DK	Deck	甲板
DO	Diesel oil	柴油
DOT	Department of Transport	美國運輸部
DP	Designated person （ISM code）	指定人員
DRK	Derrick, Crane, Winch	吊桿
DW	Dead weight	載重
DWT	Deadweight tonnage	載重噸
EC	East coast	美國東岸
ECR	Engine control room	機艙控制室
ECS	Engine control system	引擎控制系統
EEXI	Energy efficiency existing ship index	現成船能源效率
ELVENT	Electric ventilation	電力通風
EMM	Environmental management manual	環境管理手冊
(US) EPA	Environmental Protection Agency	美國環保署
ERT	Emergency response team	應急小組
ETC	Estimated time of completion	預計完成時間
ETS	Estimated time of sailing	預計航行時間
EAL	Environmentally acceptable lubricants	環保潤滑油
ECA	Emission Control Areas	排放控制區
ECS	Engine control system	柴油機控制系統
ECU	Engine control unit	柴油機控制單元
EDS	Engine diagnostics system	柴油機故障診斷系統
EEDI	Energy Efficiency Design Index	能源效率設計指標
EEOI	Energy Efficiency Operational Index	船舶能源效率營運指數
EIAPP	Engine international air pollution prevention	國際引擎空氣汙染防制
EICU	Engine interface control unit	柴油機介面控制單元
ESC	European Shippers' Council	歐洲託運人理事會

ETA	Estimated time of arrival	預計到港時間
ETB	Estimated time of berth	預計靠泊時間
ETD	Estimated time of departure	預計離港時間
F/A	Full away	出港遠颺，放大洋
FIVA	Fuel injection and exhaust valve actuation	氣缸控制閥
FP	Freezing point	凝固點
FPP	Fixed pitch propeller	定節距螺槳
FQS	Fuel quality setting	燃油品質設定
FQS	Fuel quantity sensor	噴油量偵測器
FR	Fuel rail	燃油共軌
FW	Freshwater	淡水
FWE	Finish with engine	結束用俥
FWE	Finished with engine	用俥完畢（完俥）
FAC	Fast as can (loading or discharging)	盡快（裝載或排放）
FD (FDIS)	Free discharge	開放排出
FEU	Standard 40' container	標準40呎貨櫃
FMS	Fathoms	噚
FOC	Flag of convenience	權宜國船
FYG	For your guidance	供您參考
FYI	For your information	供您參考
g/BHP-Hr	Gram per brake horsepower hour	每制動馬力小時公克數
g/kWh	Gram per kilowatt hour	每千瓦小時公克數
GT	Gross tonnage	總噸數
GO	Gas oil	汽油、高級柴油
GRT	Gross registered tonnage	註冊總噸數
H&M	Hull and machinery insurance	含船體與機器之保險
HA	Hatch	貨艙
HBL	Hydrostatically balanced loading	流體靜力附載平衡
HCFC	Hydro-chlorofluorocarbon compounds, freon 22 (R22)	氫氟氯碳化物

HFC	Hydrofluorocarbon	氫氟碳化物
HO	Hold	艙
H₂S	Hydrogen sulphide	硫化氫
HCU	Hydraulic cylinder unit	氣缸液壓驅動控制單元
HFO	Heavy fuel oil	重燃油
HMI	Human machine interface	人機界面
HPS	Hydraulic power supply	液壓動力供給單元
HVAC	Heating, ventilation and air conditioning	暖氣、通風及冷氣
IAPP	International Air Pollution Prevention	國際空氣汙染防制
ICU	Injection control unit	噴射控制單元
IFA	Intermediate fuel accumulator	中間燃油續壓器
IFO	Intermediate fuel oil	中級燃油
IG	Inert gas	惰性氣體
IGS	Inert gas system	惰氣系統
IMDG	International Maritime Dangerous Good	國際海事危險貨物
IMO	International Maritime Organization	國際海事組織
INF code	International Code for the Safe Carriage of Packaged Irradiated Nuclear Fuel, Plutonium and High-Level Radioactive Wastes on board Ships	國際危險貨物指導規則，國際危規
IOPP	International Oil Pollution Prevention	國際油汙染防制
ISSC	International Ship Security Certificate	國際船舶保全證書
ISO	International Standards Organisation	國際標準組織
KOH	Potassium hydroxide	氫氧化鉀
kW	Kilo Watt	千瓦
LF	Load factor	裝載因子
LFO	Light fuel oil	輕質燃油
LNG	Liquefied natural gas	液化天然氣
LO	Lubricating oil	潤滑油
LOA	Length overall	船全長
LPG	Liquefied petroleum gas	液化石油氣

LT	Long ton = 1016.05 kg	長噸
LCD	Load change dependent	依據負荷變化決定（汽缸油是否增量）
LFO	Light fuel oil	輕燃油
LOP	Local operation panel	現場操作面板
MDO	Marine diesel oil	船用柴油
MARPOL	International Convention on the Prevention of Pollution from Ships	防止船舶污染國際公約
MCR	Maximum continuous rating	最大連續出力
M/E	Main engine	主機
MEP	Mean effective pressure	平均有效壓力
MEPC	Maritime Environment Protection Committee	海洋環境保護委員會
MFO	Marine fuel oil	船用燃料油
MFP	Maximum firing pressure	最大點火壓力
MGO	Marine gas oil	船用輕柴油
MOP	Main operation panel	主操控電腦
MPC	Multi purpose controller	多功能控制器
MSD	Marine sanitation device	船上衛生設備
MSD	Marine sanitation devices	船用衛生裝置
M/V, MS, MV XX	Motor ship, Motor vessel	柴油主機船、油機船XX號
MT	Metric ton	公噸
MV	Motor vessel	油機船
NH₃	Ammonia	氨，阿摩尼亞，尿素
NOₓ	Nitrogen oxides	氮氧化物
NM	Nautical mile	海里
NSTM	Naval ships technical manual	（美國）海軍船舶技術手冊
N₂O	Nitrous oxide	一氧化二氮
NPSH	Net positive suction head	淨正吸入壓頭
OCM	Oil content monitors	油含量偵測器

ODMC	Oil discharge monitoring and control	油排放監控
OPS	Optimum propeller speed	最佳螺槳速率
ORB	Oil record book	油料紀錄簿
OSHA	Occupational Safety and Health Act	職業安全衛生法則
OSV	Offshore support vessel	海域（離岸）支援船
OWHT	Oily waste holding tank	含油廢料暫存櫃
OWHT	Oily waste holding tank	含油廢棄物暫存櫃
OWS	Oily water separators	油水分離器
P&I	Protection and Indemnity	保護與賠償船東保險
PCT	Percent	百分比
PG	Persian Gulf	波斯灣
ppm	Parts per million	百萬分之一
PCS	Propulsion control system	推進控制系統
PCV	Press control valve	壓力控制閥
PM	Particulate matter	粒狀物，微粒
PSC	Port state control	港口國管制
PTO	Power take off	動力輸出裝置
PTO	Power take off	輔助功率輸出裝置
RAC	Refrigeration and air conditioning	冷凍與空調
RFO	Residual fuel oil	殘餾燃油、渣油
RM	Residue marine (as used in ISO 8217)	殘渣船用燃油
RoRo	Roll-on roll-off	駛上駛下船，滾裝船
RPM	Revolution per minute	每分鐘轉數
S/B ME	Stand by main engine	主機備便
SAN	Strong acid number	強酸值
SBT	Segregated ballast tank	隔離壓載艙
SCR	Selective catalytic reduction	選擇催化（觸媒）還原
SEEMP	Ship Energy Efficiency Management Plan	船舶能效管理計畫
SFOC	Specific fuel oil consumption	燃油消耗率

SG	Specific gravity	比重
SI	International system of units	公制單位
SMG	Shaft mounted generator	軸發電機
SO₂	Sulfur dioxides	二氧化硫
SOx	Sulphurous oxides	硫氧化物
SS , SV XX	Steam ship, Steam vessel	蒸汽機船 xx 號
SSS	Super slow steaming	超低速運轉
SAR	Search and rescue	搜救
SATPM	Saturday P.M.	週六下午
SMC	Safety management certificate, ISM code	安全管理證書
SOF	Statement of facts	事實陳述
SOPEP	Shipboard oil pollution emergency plan	船上油污染應變計畫
SPM	Single point mooring	單點繫泊
SSMM	Ship safety management manual	船舶安全管理手冊
STCW	Standards of Training, Certificates and Watchkeeping	訓練、發證、當值標準
SW	Seawater	海水
SWAD	Salt water arrival draft	抵達鹹水吃水
SWDD	Salt water departure draft	離開鹹水吃水
TAN	Total acid number	總酸值
TBN	Total base number	總鹼值
T/C	Turbo charger	過給氣機，渦輪增壓機，排氣增壓機
TDC	Top dead center	上死點
TPH	Tones per hour	每小時噸數
TBT	Tributyltin, Used in tin-based antifouling	三丁基錫
TEU	Standard 20' container	20呎標準貨櫃
UMA	Unattended Machinery Area	無人當值機艙
USCG	US Coast Guard	美國海岸防衛隊
UTC	Coordinated Universal Time	世界標準時間

VCB	Vacuum circuit breaker	真空斷路器
VCM	vessel contingency manual	船舶應急手冊
VEC	Variable exhaust valve closing	可變排氣閥關閉
VF	Variable frequency	變頻
VLCC	Very large crude carrier	巨型油輪
VCU	Valve control unit	排氣閥控制單元
VEC	Variable exhaust valve closing	可變排氣閥關閉
VGP	Vessel general permit	船舶通用許可證
VI	Viscosity index	黏度指數
VIT	Variable injection timing	可變噴射正時
VTG	Variable turbocharger geometry	可變渦輪截面
WECS	Wärtsilä engine control system	瓦錫蘭機艙控制系統
W/H	Wheel house	駕駛台
WIF	Water in fuel emulsion	燃油水乳化

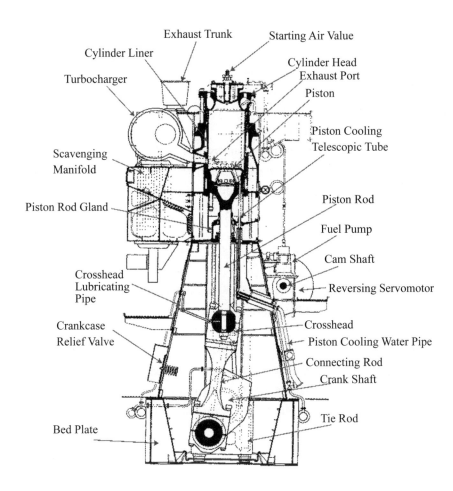

Exhaust Trunk
Starting Air Value
Cylinder Liner
Cylinder Head
Exhaust Port
Turbocharger
Piston
Piston Cooling
Telescopic Tube
Scavenging
Manifold
Piston Rod Gland
Piston Rod
Fuel Pump
Cam Shaft
Crosshead
Lubricating
Pipe
Reversing Servomotor
Crankcase
Relief Valve
Crosshead
Piston Cooling Water Pipe
Connecting Rod
Crank Shaft
Bed Plate
Tie Rod

二、柴油機（柴油引擎）（Diesel Engine）

空氣瓶	Air bottle (Air container, Air cylinder, Air reservoir)
空氣壓縮機	Air compressor
正俥凸輪	Ahead cam
正俥油缸	Ahead oil cylinder (Ahead oil bottle)
空氣分配器	Air distributor
空氣分配器凸輪	Air distributor cam
進氣閥	Air inlet valve (Suction valve)
自動停俥裝置	Automatic cut-out device

回火	Backfire
擋板	Baffle
滾珠（滾子）軸承	Ball (Roller) bearing
軸承軸瓦上半塊	Bearing bush-upper half
軸承外殼下半塊	Bearing shell-lower half
機座	Bed plate
機座橫樑	Bed plate transverse member
下死點	Bottom dead center (BDC)
二氧化碳	Carbon dioxide
一氧化碳	Carbon monoxide
燃油氣化	Carburetion
凸輪軸傳動機構	Camshaft transmission gear
離心力	Centrifugal force
鏈條傳動	Chain transmission (Chain drive)
間隙	Clearance
壓縮行程	Compression stroke
傳導係數	Conductivity coefficient
定速調速器	Constant-speed governor gear
運行控制裝置	Control device for running engine
起動控制裝置	Control device for starting
控制系統	Control system
連桿大端軸承	Connecting rod bottom end bearing (Connecting rod large end bearing)
連桿小端軸承	Connecting rod small end bearing
連桿	Connecting rod
定壓增壓系統	Constantpressure (Super) charging system
燃燒室	Combustion chamber
曲柄（拐）	Crank
曲拐軸	Crank shaft
曲軸臂	Crank arm
曲軸銷	Crank pin
曲軸頸（主軸）	Crank shaft journal (Main journal)
曲軸箱道門	Crankcase door (Crankcase manhole)
曲軸箱防爆門	Crankcase explosion door
曲軸箱防爆安全閥	Crankcase explosion relief valve

曲軸箱	Crankcase
曲柄銷軸承	Crankpin bearing
十字頭	Crosshead
十字頭銷軸承	Crosshead bearing (Crosshead pin bearing)
十字頭導板	Cross head guide (Guide rail, Guide way, Guide plate)
十字頭銷	Crosshead pin
十字頭滑塊	Crosshead shoe (Guide shoe)
十字頭式活塞	Crosshead type piston
橫流掃氣	Cross scavenging
壓縮環	Compression ring
氣缸	Cylinder
氣缸起動閥	Cylinder air starting valve
氣缸本體	Cylinder body (Block, Jacket)
氣缸蓋（氣缸頭）	Cylinder cover (Cylinder head)
氣缸套	Cylinder liner
氣缸注油器	Cylinder lubricator
微速前進（後退）	Dead slow ahead (Astern)
雙凸輪換向裝置	Double cam reversing device
半速前進（後退）	Half ahead (Astern)
全速前進（後退）	Hull ahead (Astern)
緊急全速前進（後退）	Emergency full ahead (Astern)
排氣凸輪	Exhaust cam
排氣渦輪增壓機	Exhaust gas turbocharger (Turbo-blower)
排氣總管	Exhaust manifold
排氣管	Exhaust pipe
排氣口	Exhaust port
排氣行程	Exhaust stroke
排氣閥	Exhaust valve
用俥完畢（完俥）	Finished with engine (F.W.E.)
機架	Frame (Column, Entablature)
四衝程船用柴油機	Four stroke marine diesel engine
噴油凸輪	Fuel cam
齒輪傳動	Gear transmission
活塞桿填料箱	Gland box for piston rod (Stuffing box for piston rod)
調速器	Governor

187

最高轉速調速裝置	Maximum-speed governor gear
機械式調速器	Mechanical governor
貫穿螺栓導套	Guide bush for tie rod
主起動閥手輪	Hand wheel for starting valve
缸套頂圈	Head ring for cylinder liner
高（中、低）速柴油機	High (Medium, Low) speed diesel engine
地腳螺栓	Holding down bolt (Anchor bolt)
液壓調速器	Hydraulic governor
惰輪	Idle wheel
脈衝增壓系統	Impulse pressure charging system
軸馬力	Shaft power
指示馬力	Indicated power
示功器旋塞	Indicator cock
示功圖	Indicator diagram (Card)
示功閥	Indicator valve
吸氣行程	Inlet (Suction) stroke
回（環）流掃氣	Loop scavenging
主軸承	Main bearing (Bed plate bearing)
倒掛式主軸承	Main bearing of under slung type
主軸承撐桿螺栓	Main bearing stay bolt
主起動閥	Main starting valve
機械增壓	Mechanical supercharging
安全閥	Safety valve
頂桿	Tappet rod
二衝程船用柴油機	Two stroke marine diesel engine
刮油環	Oil scraper ring (Oil ring, Scraper ring)
佈油環	Oil distributing ring
活塞	Piston
活塞頂（頭，冠）	Piston crown (Head)
活塞冷卻水管	Piston cooling pipe
活塞本體	Piston body
活塞銷	Piston pin (Gudgeon pin)
活塞環	Piston ring
活塞環槽	Piston ring groove
活塞桿	Piston rod

活塞桿凸緣	Piston rod flange
活塞裙	Piston skirt
掃氣口	Scavenging port
掃氣道	Scavenging belt (Trunk)
氣孔掃氣	Port scavenging
氣孔氣閥掃氣	Port-valve scavenging
動力（作功）行程	Power (Working) stroke
填料函壓環	Pressure ring for stuffing box
貫穿螺栓護蓋	Protecting covering for tie rod
挺桿	Push rod
往復管	Reciprocating pipe
倒轉	Reverse
換向控制桿	Reversing control lever
換向桿	Reversing lever
搖臂	Rocker arm (Rocking lever)
轉向指示器	Running direction indicator
填料函刮油環	Scraper ring for stuffing box
填料函密封環	Sealing ring for stuffing box
單凸輪換向裝置	Single cam reversing device
慢速正俥（倒俥）	Slow ahead (Astern)
鏈輪	Sprocket (Sprocket wheel)
起動空氣控制閥	Starting air control valve
起動空氣導閥	Starting air pilot valve
起動空氣管	Starting air pipe
起動凸輪	Starting cam
起動裝置	Starting device
起動手柄	Starting lever (Starting handle)
起動閥連鎖裝置	Starting valve blocking device
起動閥	Starting valve
分級（塔形）活塞	Stepped piston
單（複）式增壓系統	Single (Complex) type super- charging system
填料函殼體	Stuffing box casing
活塞桿填料函	Stuffing box for piston rod
填料函壓蓋	Stuffing box gland
並聯增壓	Supercharging in parallel system

189

輪機英文

串聯增壓	Supercharging in series system
增壓系統	Supercharging system (Pressure charging system)
伸縮管	Telescope pipe
填料函張力彈簧	Tension spring for stuffing box
貫穿螺栓（繫桿）	Throughbolt (Tierod, Tiebolt) through-going-tie-bolt
推力軸承	Thrust bearing
推力塊	Thrust pad
推力軸	Thrust shaft
筒形活塞	Trunk piston
定時圖	Timing diagram
上死點	Top dead center (TDC)
轉俥機	Turning gear
二級增壓	Two-stage supercharging
直（單）流掃氣	Uniflow scavenging
氣閥傳動機構	Valve driving mechanism
全制式調速裝置	Variable-speed governor gear
變（動）壓增壓系統	Variable (pulse) pressure charging system
耐磨環	Wearing ring

三、燃油與滑油（Fuel and Lubricating Oil）

添加劑	Additive
鋁含量	Aluminum content
灰分	Ash content
瀝青	Asphalt
軸承潤滑	Bearing lubrication
增壓泵	Booster pump
丁烷	Butane
熱值	Calorific value
殘炭值	Carbon residue
十六烷數	Cetane number
滑油循環櫃	Circulating lube oil tank
濁點	Cloud point
調節控制桿	Control lever for adjusting oil
調節齒桿	Control rack (Toothed control rod)

調節齒圈	Control sleeve (Control pinion)
腐蝕	Corrosion
氣缸潤滑	Cylinder lubrication
日用櫃	Daily service tank
柴油指數	Diesel index
蒸餾的範圍	Distilling range
雙層底油艙	Double bottom fuel tank
乾油底殼式潤滑	Dry oil sump type lubrication
雙聯細濾器	Dual oil filter (Duplex oil filter)
極壓添加劑	Extreme pressure additive
細濾器	Filter
閃點	Flash point
冰點	Freezing point
排油閥	Fuel delivery valve
高壓油泵	Fuel injection pump
（燃油噴射泵）	
噴油器殼體	Fuel injector holder (Fuel injector housing)
噴油器、燃油閥	Fuel injector, fuel valve
進油孔	Fuel inlet hole
燃油系統	Fuel oil system
油壓調節閥	Fuel pressure regulating valve
油量調節機構	Fuel regulating linkage
回油孔	Fuel return hole
沉澱櫃	Fuel settling tank
燃油駁運泵	Fuel transfer pump
油品等級	Grade of oil
加熱器	Heater
高壓油管	High pressure fuel pipe
發火品質	Ignition quality
噴油嘴	Injection nozzle
中間燃料油	Internal fuel oil
滑油冷卻器	Lube oil cooler
滑油泵	Lube oil pump
滑油粗濾器	Lube oil strainer
潤滑系統	Lubricating system

船用柴油	Marine diesel oil (MDO)
船用燃料油	Marine fuel oil (MFO)
船用輕柴油	Marine gas oil (MGO)
機械雜質	Mechanical impurities
低壓潤滑系統	Low pressure lubrication system
針閥	Needle valve
集油井（櫃）	Oil head tank
油孔	Oil orifice oil hole
分油機	Oil separator
污油櫃	Oil sludge tank
氣缸注油器	Oil squirt (Cylinder lubricator)
貯油箱	Oil storage tank
集油箱	Oil sump (Sump tank, Crank bilge)
油道	Oil way (Oil channel)
溢流管	Overflow pipe
抗氧化安定性	Oxidation resistance
柱塞套筒	Plunger guide
柱塞式噴油泵	Plunger type fuel injection pump (Bosch fuel injection pump)
柱塞（芯子）	Plunger
傾（澆）點，流動點	Pour point
保壓閥	Pressure retaining valve
油泵行程調節桿	Regulating lever for pump stroke
沉澱物	Sediment
比重	Specific gravity
回油閥式高壓油泵	Spill valve type fuel injection pump
針閥頂桿	Spindle
飛濺潤滑	Splash lubrication
蒸汽加熱器	Steam heater
蒸汽加熱盤管	Steam heating coil
蒸汽加熱管	Steam heating pipe
粗濾器	Strainer
強酸值	Strong acid number (SAN)
吸油管	Suction duct (Suction line)
進油閥（回油閥）	Suction valve (Spill valve, Blowthrough valve)

硫分	Sulphur content
三通閥	Three way valve
總酸值	Total acid number (TAN)
總鹼值	Total base number (TBN)
釩含量	Vanadium content
黏度指數	Viscosity index
黏度	Viscosity
水分	Water content
濕集油箱式潤滑	Wet oil sump type lubrication

四、泵及泵送系統（Pump and Pumping System）

出灰泵	Ash-ejecting pump
軸向柱塞泵	Axial plunger pump
軸流泵	Axial-flow pump
壓載泵	Ballast pump
艙底水泵	Bilge pump
鹽（鹵）水泵	Brine pump
蝶形閥	Butterfly valve
集中引水系統	Central priming system (CPS)
離心泵	Centrifugal pump
循環泵	Circulating pump (Evacuation pump)
旋塞（考克）	Cock
凝水泵	Condensate pump
定量泵	Constant displacement pump (Constant delivery pump)
冷卻水泵	Cooling water pump
擴散管	Diffuser
蒸汽直接作用泵	Direct-acting steam pump
排出口	Discharge (Delivery)
容積式泵	Displacement pump
輔給水泵	Donkey feed water pump
雙作用葉片泵	Double-acting vane pump
雙作用泵	Double-acting pump
雙級泵	Double-stage pump
雙缸泵	Duplex pump

噴射泵	Ejector pump (Ejector)
給水泵	Feed water pump
消防泵	Fire pump (Fire fighting pump)
淡水泵	Fresh water pump
閘板閥	Gate valve
齒輪泵	Gear pump
油壓泵	Hydraulic pump
噴射式泵	Jet pump
通用泵	General service pump (Service pump)
球形閥	Globe valve
臥式泵	Horizontal pump
液壓泵	Hydraulic pump
葉輪	Impeller (Vane wheel)
內齒輪泵	Inside gearing pump
流道	Liquid path
主機驅動泵	Main-engine-driven pump
電動泵	Motor-driven pump
淨正吸入壓頭	Net positive suction head (NPSH)
止回閥	Non-return valve (Check valve)
非自吸式泵	Non-self priming pump
外齒輪泵	Outside gearing pump
管路	Pipe line
活塞泵	Piston pump
柱塞泵	Plunger pump
引水泵	Priming pump (Primer pump)
泵體	Pump body
泵浦特性曲線	Pump characteristic curve
泵缸	Pump cylinder
泵殼	Pump housing
泵缸套	Pump liner
速閉閥	Quick closing valve (Strip valve)
徑向柱塞泵	Radial plunger pump
徑流泵	Radial-flow pump
往復泵	Reciprocating pump
釋壓閥	Relief valve

轉閥	Rotary (Rotating) valve
迴轉泵	Rotary pump
衛生水泵	Sanitary pump
螺桿泵	Screw pump
自吸式泵	Self-priming pump
污水泵	Sewage pump
單缸泵	Simplex pump
單作用泵	Single-acting pump
單作用葉片泵	Single-acting vane pump
單級泵	Single-stage pump
滑閥	Slide (Sliding) valve
填料箱	Stuffing box
吸入口	Suction (Eye)
吸入閥	Suction valve
系統水頭損失	System head loss
傳送泵	Transfer pump
旋渦泵	Turbine pump
真空泵	Vacuum pump
閥	Valve
葉片泵	Vane pump
變量泵	Variable displacement pump (Variable delivery pump)
立式泵	Vertical pump
蝸殼	Volute
水環泵	Water ring pump

五、電力系統（Power System）

空氣斷路器	Air circuit breaker (ACB)
真空斷路器	Vacuum circuit breaker (VCB)
電流錶	Ammeter
放大器	Amplifier
滅弧罩	Arc shield
電樞	Armature
非同步電動機	Asynchronous motor
自動斷路器	Automatic circuit breaker (ACB)

自動調頻調載器	Automatic frequency and load regulator
自動分載裝置	Automatic load-sharing device
自動電壓調節器	Automatic voltage regulator (AVR)
鎮流器	Ballast
蓄電池系統	Battery system
斷路器	Breaker
匯流排	Bus bar
換向器（整流器）	Commutator
複激	Compound-wound
電容器	Capacitor
接線盒	Connection box
接觸器	Contactor
操縱（控制）臺	Control platform
藕合變壓器	Couple transformer
斷流器	Cut-out
配電箱（盤、板）	Distribution board
雙刀開關	Double pole switch
電磁式發電機	Elector-magnetic generator
電刷	Electric brush
頻率錶	Frequency meter
頻率	Frequency
發電機面板	Generator panel
發電機	Generator
同相	In phase
限止開關	Limit switch
配電板	Load-dispatching board (Switch board)
激磁場線圈	Magnetic field coil
主配電板	Main switch board
電動機（馬達）	Motor
失壓保護	No-voltage protection
缺相保護	Open-phase protection
超載斷路器	Over load circuit breaker
過電流保護	Over-current protection
超載保護	Over-load protection
超載開關	Overload switch

併俥操作	Parallel operation
併俥開關	Paralleling switch
相位	Phase
原動機	Prime motor
保護裝置	Protection device
電抗器	Reactor
整流器	Rectifier
繼電器	Relay
電阻器	Resistor
逆功率保護	Reverse power protection
轉子	Rotor
區域配電板	Section board
自激	Self-excited
串激（繞）	Series-wound
岸電接線箱	Shore connection box
短路電流保護	Short circuit current protection
並激（繞）	Shunt-wound
鼠籠式電動機	Squirrel cage motor
起動器	Starter
定子	Stator
供電網	Supply network
開關	Switch
同步感應電動機	Synchronous induction motor
同步指示器（儀）	Synchroscope
試驗板	Test board
三相電動機	Three-phase motor
變壓器	Transformer
跳脫裝置	Trip device
欠（低）壓保護	Under-voltage protection
電壓錶	Voltmeter
功率錶	Wattmeter

六、淨油機（Purifier）

分離筒本體	Bowl body

分離盤	Bowl discs
分離筒蓋	Bowl hood
分離筒轉軸	Bowl spindle
離心機（即淨油機）	Centrifuge
潔油機	Clarifier
粗粒化	Coalesce
錐形盤	Conical plates
阻水環	Damp ring
擋水器	Demister
沖洗水	Flushing water
機架壓蓋	Frame cap
比重環（重力環）	Gravity disc
離心分油機	Oil centrifuge
擋油圈	Oil deflector
疏油閥	Oil drain valve
油位顯示器	Oil level indicator
除油閥	Oil recovery valve
分油機	Oil separator
滑動圈	Operating slide
工作水	Operating water
分水盤	Paring disc
除渣閥	Scum valve
分離筒	Separator bowl
沉澱櫃	Settling tank
活動底盤	Sliding bowl bottom
污渣出口	Sludge outlet
油泥櫃	Sludge tank

七、船用鍋爐（Marine Boiler）

空氣調溫器	Air attemperator
調風門	Air damper
空氣擴散盤	Air diffuser disk
導流器	Air director
調風器	Air register

空氣調節器	Air regulator (Air register)
擋煙牆	Baffle wall
風機	Blower
爐衣	Boiler clothing (Boiler lagging)
沸水管	Boiling-water tube
底部排污閥	Bottom blow down valve
低位水位計	Bottom water level gauge
霧化器	Burner atomizer (Sprayer)
噴油嘴	Burner tip (Nozzle)
風箱	Burner wind box
煙囪	Chimney (Funnel)
有肋的盤管	Coil tube with ribs
盤管強制循環廢氣鍋爐	Coil-tube forced-circulation exhaust boiler
旋風汽水分離器	Cyclone steam separator
筒形鍋爐	Cylindrical boiler (Shell type boiler)
除氧器	Deaerator
減（降）熱器	Desuperheater
下降（導）管	Downcomer
風口	Draught door
鼓筒形鍋爐	Drum boiler
節熱器	Economizer
廢氣（熱）鍋爐	Exhaust boiler
給水止回閥	Feed water check valve
給水離子交換器	Feed water ion exchanger
給水截止閥	Feed water stop valve
給水閥	Feed water valve
爐排	Fire bar (Fire grate)
爐門	Fire door
火口	Fire hole (Combustion head)
火（水）管鍋爐	Fire (Water) tube boiler
耐火磚襯層	Fire-brick lining
火焰檢測器	Flame detector
強制通風機	Force draught fan
前部聯箱	Front header
爐膛	Furnace (Fire box)

199

爐膽	Furnace flue
鍋爐煙道	Furnace uptake
爐牆	Furnace wall
玻璃水位表	Glass water lever gauge
手調風門	Hand regulating throttle
臥式三回程火管鍋爐	Horizontal triple-pass fire tube boiler
熱水循環泵	Hot water regulating pump
熱水井	Hot well
點火器	Igniter
點火噴油嘴	Ignition nozzle
點火變壓器	Ignition transformer
進口分配聯箱	Inlet distributing header
內給水管	Internal feed pipe
下部聯箱	Lower header
低水位報警器	Low-water level alarm
低水位切斷裝置	Low-water level cut-off device
人孔門	Manhole door
噴油嘴體	Nozzle holder
噴孔	Nozzle hole (Nozzle orifice)
噴油嘴管架	Nozzle support
燃燒器	Oil burner
燃油預熱器	Oil preheater
燃油式輔鍋爐	Oil-burning auxiliary boiler
出口分配聯箱	Outlet distributing header
光滑管	Plain tube
預燃室	Precombustion chamber
壓力比例調節器	Pressure ratio regulator
比例操作器	Proportional ratio apparatus
後部聯箱	Rear header
水冷壁	Rear water wall tube
遠距離水位指示計	Remote water level indicator
上升管	Riser tube
浮渣盤	Scum disk
風門調節伺服器	Servomotor for throttle regulation
側水冷壁	Side water wall tube

單層盤管	Single-layer tube
波形管	Sinuflo tube
煙箱	Smoke chamber (Smoke box)
煙道	Smoke flue
煙管	Smoke tube
吹灰器	Soot blower
霧化片	Sprayer plate
牽條管	Stay tube
牽條	Stay
除水器	Steam trap
蒸汽分配器	Steam distributor
汽鼓	Steam drum
汽水分離器	Steam purifier (Steam separator)
集汽管	Steam receiver
停汽閥	Steam stop valve
蒸汽匯集器	Steaming header
直（橫、彎、盤） 管鍋爐	Straight (Cross, Bent, Coil, Thimble) tube boiler
過熱器	Superheater
支撐管	Support tube
上排污（吹放）閥	Surface blow-down valve
表面（底部）吹放閥	Surface (Bottom) blow-off valve
旋渦室	Swirl chamber
麻花管	Swirlyflo tube
風門	Throttle (Air intake flap)
管式鍋爐	Tubular boiler
上部聯箱	Upper header
立式橫煙管鍋爐	Vertical fire tube boiler
立（臥）式鍋爐	Vertical (Horizontal) boiler
水鼓	Water drum
水管聯箱	Water header
水位調節器	Water level regulator
水位計分支閥	Water level root valve
水位表	Water lever gauge
水處理	Water treatment

201

水冷牆	Water-cooled wall (Water screen, Water wall)
水管鍋爐	Water tube boiler

八、造水機（Fresh water generator, Distiller, Distillation plant, Desalination plant）

空蝕	Cavitation
檢驗旋塞	Check cock
冷凝器	Condenser
凝水泵	Distillate pump
蒸發器	Evaporator
急遽汽化（閃化）室	Flash chamber
鹽度計	Salinity indicator

九、冷凍與空調（Refrigeration and Air Conditioning）

空氣濾清器	Air cleaner
空調	Air conditioning
空氣調節機	Air conditioner
空氣冷卻器	Air cooler
空氣乾燥室	Air drying chamber
空氣加熱器	Air heater
風管	Air pipe
風冷式冷凝器	Air-cooled condenser
自動液壓控制裝置	Automatic hydraulic capacity control device
自動水量調節閥	Automatic water regulating valve
背壓調節閥	Back-pressure valve
波紋管（風箱）	Bellows
鹽（鹵）水冷卻	Brine refrigeration
艙室溫度控制器	Cabin type temperature control
調量器	Capacity regulator
毛細管	Capillary tube
中央空調系統	Central air conditioning system
充液閥	Charging valve
冷藏	Cold storage

壓縮機	Compressor
冷凝器	Condenser
冷凝器進入閥	Condenser inlet valve
冷凝器出液閥	Condenser outlet valve
冷卻盤管	Cooling coil
臨界溫度	Critical temperature
擋水曲板	Curve flap
出液閥	Delivery valve
膜片	Diaphragm
壓差控制	Differential pressure control
排氣融霜管	Discharge defrost pipe
雙閥座截止閥	Double seat stop valve
乾燥器	Drier/Dryer
蒸發盤管	Evaporator coil tube
蒸發器	Evaporator
膨脹閥	Expansion valve
散熱鰭片	Fin
浮動式自動回油閥	Floating type automatic oil return valve
氟化烴	Fluorinated hydrocarbon
氟里昂	Freon
波形散熱片	Gill
探漏燈（鹵素燈）	Halide lamp
手動容量控制閥	Hand capacity control valve
熱交換器	Heat exchanger
熱泵式空調機	Heat-pump air conditioner
高速誘導式空調系統	High speed induction air conditioning system
高壓繼電器	High voltage relay
加濕器	Humidifier
濕度調節器	Humidistat
濕度控制器	Humidity controller
壓縮機泵的進口段	Inducer
進風柵	Inlet grid
油位檢查鏡	Inspection glass for oil level
隔熱艙	Insulate hold
中間冷卻器	Intercooler

內部均壓裝置	Internal equalizer
液位控制	Liquid level control
貯液器	Liquid receiver
液體分離器	Liquid separator
船用臭氧發生器	Marine ozonizer
油預熱器	Oil preheater
油分離器	Oil separator
回油裝置	Oil-return device
閥孔隙	Orifice
外平衡管	Outer balance pipe
出風柵	Outlet grid
出液管	Outlet pipe
溫包式溫度控制器	Phial type temperature controller
（強制）通風系統	Plenum
氣動薄膜蝶閥	Pneumatic film flap valve
毛髮式氣動濕度控制器	Pneumatic hair humidity controller
壓力控制	Pressure control
直接冷媒	Primary refrigerant
散熱盤管	Radiator coil tube
散熱器	Radiator
冷媒瓶	Refrigerant bottle
冷媒	Refrigerant
冷凍	Refrigeration
再加熱盤管	Reheating coil
回氣管	Return pipe
二次空調系統	Secondary air conditioning system
間接冷媒	Secondary refrigerant
半導體空調機	Semi-conductor air conditioner
半封閉式壓縮機	Semi-enclosed compressor
感溫（球）包	Sensing bulb
單風管系統	Single duct system
電磁閥	Solenoid valve
吸入截止閥	Suction stop valve
吸入濾網	Suction strainer
終端加熱器	Terminal-heater

熱電制冷器	Thermoelectric refrigeration
恒溫器	Thermostat
熱力膨脹閥	Thermostatic expansion valve
節流閥	Throttle valve
頂式通風機	Top ventilator
翅片管	Tuberculate(d) pipe
雙風管系統	Twin duct system
卸荷缸	Unloading cylinder
蒸氣壓縮循環	Vapor-compression cycle
通風	Ventilation
通風機	Ventilator
水量調節閥	Water regulating valve
窗式空調機	Window-type air conditioner
分區加熱器	Zone heater

十、甲板機械（Deck Machineries）

錨	Anchor
錨鏈	Anchor chain
錨機	Anchor windlass
輔助手柄	Auxiliary lever
輔助閥	Auxiliary valve
軸向雙斜盤式油馬達	Axial double-tilting frame type oil motor
帶式煞車	Band brake
吊貨杆	Boom (Derrick boom)
鏈條制動器	Cable stopper
絞盤筒	Capstan barrel
絞盤	Capstan
起貨裝置	Cargo handling gear
貨物定位裝置	Cargo spotter
起貨絞車（絞纜機）	Cargo winch
中央閥	Center valve
錨鏈捲筒	Chain drum
錨鏈輪	Chain lifter (Cable lifter, Cable holder)
鏈輪止動器	Chain lifter brake

錨鏈艙	Chain locker
換向閥	Change-over valve (Change valve)
定距螺槳	Constant pitch propeller
電液	Electro-hydraulic
電磁	Electro-magnetic
變數泵閉式系統	Closed oil system of the variable delivery pump
離合器	Clutch
操縱系統	Control system
起重機	Crane
阻尼孔	Damper hole
差動型限位開關	Differential limit switch
差動油缸	Differential oil cylinder
差動活塞	Differential piston
方向控制閥	Direction control valve
雙路油壓自鎖閥	Double-circuit oil pressure self-closing valve
應急手動操縱裝置	Emergency hand control device
回饋桿	Feed back rod
定葉	Fixed vane
浮動桿	Floating lever
浮動環	Floating ring
流量控制閥	Flow control valve
廚房	Galley
節流閥	Throttle valve
調速閥	Speed-regulating valve
槓桿回饋式從動機構	Follow-up system of the mechanical lever feedback type
齒輪式油馬達	Gear-type oil motor
手動旁通閥	Hand by-pass valve
手動截止閥	Hand stop valve (Hand cut-off valve)
高速小扭矩油馬達	High speed low torque oil motor
液壓放大器	Hydraulic amplifier
液壓馬達	Hydraulic motor
液壓油缸	Hydraulic oil cylinder
液壓泵	Hydraulic pump
吊臂	Jib (Crane jib)

吊臂止動器	Jib stopper
低速大扭矩油馬達	Low speed high torque oil motor
俯仰絞纜機	Luffing winch
主閥	Main valve
機械制動器	Mechanical brake
配油殼	Oil distribution casing
配油盤	Oil distribution disc
配油口	Oil distribution port
配油軸	Oil distribution shaft
配油套	Oil distribution sleeve
配油閥	Oil distribution valve
止回閥	One-way valve (Check valve)
直角閥	Angle valve
直通閥	Straight valve
定量泵開式系統	Open oil system of the constant delivery pump
工況選擇閥	Operating mode selector valve
擺動油缸	Oscillating oil cylinder
溢流閥	Overflow valve
先導閥	Pilot valve
壓力控制閥	Pressure control valve
減壓閥	Pressure-reducing valve
徑向柱塞泵	Radial plunger pump
徑向柱塞式油馬達	Radial-plunger-type oil motor
柱塞式舵機	Ram type steering gear
旋轉閥（滑閥）	Rotary valve (Slide valve)
三位四通閥	Three-position four-way valve
旋轉輪葉型舵機	Rotary vane type steering gear
旋轉輪葉	Rotary vane
旋轉輪葉型油缸	Rotary-vane-type oil cylinder
舵葉	Rudder blade
舵托（承）	Rudder carrier
舵柱	Rudder post
舵桿	Rudder stock
舵柄	Rudder tiller
密封條	Sealing strip

輪機英文

自鎖閥	Self-locking valve
順序閥	Sequence valve
穩定器（翼）	Stabilizer
舵機	Steering gear
伺服活塞	Servo-piston
防索鬆保護器	Slack wire protection
旋轉底盤	Slewing rim
旋轉絞車	Slewing winch
定子（葉）	Stator
止浪閥	Storm valve
傾斜盤	Swash plate
遙控操舵裝置	Telemotor steering gear
節流（槽）縫隙	Throttle slot
吊揚索（千斤索）	Topping lift
帶纜捲筒	Warping drum
錨機	Windlass

十一、軸系及推進系統（Shafting and Propulsion System）

可調螺距螺旋槳	Adjustable pitch (Variable pitch) propeller
船艏部螺旋槳	Bow propeller
定槳葉螺旋槳	Fixed-blade propeller
中間軸	Intermediate shaft (Tunnel shaft)
導邊空蝕	Leading edge cavitation
左（右）螺旋槳	Left (Right) handed propeller
鐵梨木軸承	Lignum vitae bearing
液位探測電極	Liquid level electronic probe
單環推力軸承 （密歇爾推力軸承）	Mitchell thrust bearing
壓力面空蝕	Pressure-face cavitation (Face cavitation)
推進器（螺槳）	Propeller
槳葉	Propeller blade
槳轂	Propeller boss (Propeller hub)
螺旋槳空蝕	Propeller-cavitation

軸承	Shaft bearing
軸系	Shafting
單環推力軸承	Single collar (Thrust) bearing
單環推力軸	Single collar thrust shaft
艉軸管軸承	Stem tube bearing (Stem bearing)
吸力面空蝕	Suction-face cavitation
艉軸	Tail shaft (Tube shaft)
推力軸承	Thrust block
推力環	Thrust collar
推力塊（單塊）	Thrust pad
推力軸	Thrust shaft
傳動軸	Transmission shaft
橫向推進器	Transverse propeller
支撐軸承（中間軸軸承）	Tunnel bearing (Intermediate shaft bearing)
真空沸騰式造水機	Vacuum boiling evaporator
水潤滑軸承	Water-lubricated bearing
白合金軸承	White metal bearing

209

十二、輪機用詞（Terminology for Marine Engineering）

報告溫度與壓力等狀態	
Temperature...degree centigrade, Celsius (Fahrenheit).	溫度……攝氏（華氏）……度
Sea water temperature...Celsius.	海水溫度為攝氏……度
Temperature...degree above/below normal.	溫度高／低於正常值……度
Exhuaust temperature of No.... cylinder is 3 degree above normal.	……號缸排氣溫度比正常值高出3度
...temperature/pressure critical.	……的溫度／壓力達危險
Piston cooling water temperature critical.	活塞冷卻水溫達危險
(Pump) Suction/Deliver pressure ... bars	（泵）入口／出口壓力……巴
Pressure...bars below normal.	壓力低於正常值……巴
Pressure...bars above normal.	壓力高於正常值……巴
Pressure critical.	壓力達危險

報告某艙液位	
Ballast/Fresh water/Fuel oil/Lubricating oil/Slop sounding is...metres / cubic metres.	壓艙水／淡水／燃油／滑油／污液（油）艙的液位深……公尺／立方公尺
Sounding of port side No.1 fuel oil tank ... metres.	左舷1號燃油艙液位深……公尺
Sounding of starboard side No.2 ballast tank ... centimetres.	右舷2號壓載艙深……公分
報告主機與輔機運轉狀況	
Main engine RPM...	主機轉速每分鐘……轉
Main engine output...kiloWatts.	主機出力……千瓦
No.1 auxiliary engine output... kiloWatts.	1號發電機引擎出力……千瓦
Pitch of propeller(s)...degrees.	推進器螺距……度
No problem with...	……沒問題
No problem with air compressor.	空壓機沒問題
Problem with...	……有問題
Problem with main engine.	主機有問題
Call Watch Egineer (If problems continue).	呼叫當值輪機員（如問題仍持續）
報告燃油、壓艙水等泵送情況	
No pumping at present.	目前無泵送
Filling port side No.1 double bottom tank.	正壓戴左舷1號雙層底艙
Discharged port side No.1 double bottom tank(s).	已排出左舷1號雙層底艙
Discharging port side No.2 tanks.	左舷2號艙排出中
Transferred fuel/ballast /fresh water/oil from No....tank to No....tank.	已轉駁燃油／壓艙水／淡水／油從（艙號）……艙至（艙號）……艙
Require further generator to operate additional pump(s).	需要增加發電機以運轉更多泵
簡報特殊機器事故及修理	
Breakdown of main engine(s) (at...°UTC / local time).	（在……UTC（世界協調時）／當地時間）主機故障

Total blackout from...(to...UTC / local time).	（在……ＵＴＣ／當地時間）……處電力跳脫
Blackout in...from...to...UTC / local time.	從……至……在……UTC／當地時間……處電力跳脫
Main engine stopped...at...UTC / local time due to...	因為……從……UTC／當地時間主機停止運轉
Call Master / Chief Engineer if revolutions of main engine(s) below...RPM.	如果主機轉速低於每分鐘……轉，呼叫船長／輪機長
Call Master / Chief Engineer / Watch Engineer if…	如果……，呼叫船長／輪機長／當值輪機員

* Temps Universel Coordonné, Universal Coordinated Time.

駕駛台用俥對話	
Pilot on the bridge.	引水人（領港）在駕駛台
Propulsion system.	推進系統
Is engine diesel or turbine?	主機為柴油機或透平（蒸汽渦輪）機？
Engine is diesel.	主機為柴油機
Engine is turbine.	主機為透平機
Is engine room manned?	機艙有人當值嗎？
Is engine on bridge control?	駕駛台操俥嗎？
Engine room manned.	機艙有人當值
Engine on bridge control.	主機在駕駛台操控
How long does it take to change engine from ahead to astern?	主機從進俥改為倒俥需要多少時間？
It takes...minutes to change engine from ahead to astern.	從前進轉為倒俥需要……分鐘
How long does it take to start engine from stopped?	主機從停俥到啟動需多少時間？
It takes...seconds to start engine (from stopped).	啟動主機（從停俥）需要……秒鐘
Is extra power available in emergency?	應急時有額外電力嗎？
Yes, extra power available.	是，有額外電力
No, extra power not available.	不，無額外置力

Do you have controllable or fixed pitch propeller?	貴船推進器為可變螺距式或固定螺距式？
Do you have controllable or fixed pitch propeller?	貴船推進器為可變螺距式或固定螺距式？
We have controllable pitch propeller.	本船為可變螺距推進器
We have fixed pitch propeller.	本船為固定螺距推進器
Do you have right-hand or left-hand propeller?	貴船推進器為左旋或右旋？
We have right-hand propeller.	本船為右旋推進器
We have left-hand propeller.	本船為左旋推進器
Do you have single propeller or twin propellers?	貴船為單俥或雙俥？
We have single propeller.	本船為單俥
We have twin propellers.	本船為雙俥
Do you have bow thruster or stern thruster?	貴船有艏側推進器或艉側推進器嗎？
We have bow thruster.	本船有艏側推進器
We have stern thruster.	本船有艉側推進器
We have thrusters.	本船有側推進器
What is maximum manoeuvring power ahead?	最大進俥機動操縱出力為何？
Maximum manoeuvring power ahead...kiloWatts.	最大進俥機動操縱出力……千瓦
What is maximum manoeuvring power astern?	最大倒俥機動操縱出力為多少？
Maximum manoeuvring power astern...kiloWatts.	最大倒俥機動操縱出力……千瓦
What are maximum revolutions ahead / astern?	最大進俥／倒俥轉數為多少？
Maximum revolutions ahead / astern...	最大進俥／倒俥轉數……
Do twin propellers turn inward or outward when going ahead?	前進時雙推進器為內旋或外旋
Twin propellers turn inward (When going ahead).	（前進時）雙推進器內旋
Twin propellers turn outward (When going ahead).	（前進時）雙推進器外旋

浸水狀況應變	
Use tarpaulins/... (in...).	（在……）使用防水布／……
Send diver(s) to check leak and report.	派潛水夫檢查洩漏處，並回報
Stop leak from inside/outside (...space/area).	從（艙間／區域）內側／外側堵漏
Stopping leak from inside/outside not possible.	不可能從內／外側堵漏
Leak stopped.	漏水已停

Cancellation of alarm.	解除警報
Is flooding stopped?	浸水已停止了嗎？
Flooding (in...) stopped.	在……浸水已停止
No flooding (in...) not completely stopped (yet).	在……浸水尚未完全停止
Is flooding under control?	浸水控制住了嗎？
Yes, flooding (in...) under control.	是，在……正浸水，已控制住
Flooding (in...) below capacity of (bilge) pump(s).	在……正浸水低於（艙底水泵）容量
Flooding restricted to...space/area.	浸水侷限於……艙間／區域
Post damage control watches and report.	布署損管警戒，並回報
Damage control watches post (in...).	（在……）損管警戒已布署
How much water is in vessel?	多少水進入船內
Amount of water (in...) about...tonnes.	（在……）水量大約……噸
(Bilge) Pump(s) remain on stand by.	（艙底水）泵維持備便
(Bilge) Pump(s) standing by.	（艙底水）泵正在備便
Engine room remains on stand by.	機艙仍然維持備便
Engine room standing by.	機艙正備便
Additional emergency generator remains on stand by.	額外的緊急發電機仍保持備便
Emergency generator No....standing by.	第……號緊急發電機正備便中
Damage control team remain on stand by.	請損管班維持備便
Damage control team is standing by.	損管班正在備便
Rope-off flooded area.	放繩索入浸水區
Flooded area roped-off.	浸水區域已放入繩索
Check leak every...minutes/ hour(s) and report.	每……分鐘／小時檢視洩漏處，並回報
Leak checked—no flooding.	已檢視洩漏處，無浸水
Leak checked—minor / major flooding (in...).	洩漏處已檢視（在……）輕微／嚴重浸水
Flooding stopped.	浸水已停
Alarm cancelled.	解除警報
Alarm cancelled, with following restrictions...	在下列限制下……警報解除

擱淺狀況應變	
Reporting groundings and ordering immediate actions.	報告擱淺並下令立即行動
Vessel aground. Stop engine.	船發生擱淺。停俥
Close watertight doors and report.	關閉水密門，並回報
Watertight doors closed.	水密門已關閉
Is vessel still making way ahead/astern?	船是否仍向前／後行駛？
Yes, vessel making way ahead/astern.	是，船還在向前／後行駛
No, vessel not making way.	不，船已動不了
Give vessel aground signal.	發出船艙擱淺信號
Hoist vessel aground signal.	懸掛「船擱淺」信號
"Vessel aground" signal hoisted.	「船擱淺」信號已懸掛
Switch on "vessel aground" lights.	開啟船舶擱淺號誌燈
"Vessel aground" lights switched on.	船舶擱淺號誌燈已開
Sounding "vessel aground" gong/ whistle signal.	發出「船擱淺」鈴／鐘／汽笛信號
Inform engine room.	通知機艙
Engine room informed.	已通知機艙
What part is aground?	何部位擱淺？
Vessel aground forward.	船前部擱淺
Vessel aground amidships.	船舯部擱淺
Vessel aground aft.	船後部擱淺
Vessel aground full length.	全船擱淺
Stand by fore and aft.	船艏船艉就布屬
Forward station/Aft station standing by.	船艏船艉站正在備便
Stand by port anchor / starboard anchor.	備便左右船錨
Port anchor / Starboard anchor standing by.	左右船錨正在備便
船受損應變	
Where is position?	船位在何處？
Position...	船位在……
Reporting damage.	損壞報告
What is damage?	損壞如何？

No damage.	無損壞
Crack in plating.	船板有裂縫
Crack in No....double bottom.	在第……雙重底有裂縫
Crack in No....hold(s) cargo hold(s).	在第……貨艙／液貨艙有裂縫
Crack in fuel pipe(s).	燃油管有裂縫
Crack(s) in main/ auxiliary engine(s) foundation.	在主／輔機基座有裂縫
Crack(s) in...	在……有裂縫
Deformation/Indentation(s) to plating.	船板變形／凹陷
Deformation(s)/Indentation(s) to...	……變形／凹陷
Check flooding and report.	檢視浸水，並回報
No flooding.	無浸水
Flooding in...	在……（部位）浸水
Is danger imminent?	有立即危險嗎？
No, danger not imminent.	沒有，無立即危險
Yes, danger of decreasing stability.	有，有穩度降低的危險
Yes, danger of damage by sea.	有，有浪損的危險
Yes, danger of breaking apart.	有，有裂斷的危險
Yes, danger of pollution.	有，有污染的危險
Yes, danger of...	有，有……的危險
What is nature of sea bottom?	海底性質為何？
Close all openings and report.	請關閉所有開口，並回報
All openings closed.	所有開口已關閉
Openings in engine room closed.	機艙開口已關閉
Openings in hold(s)/tank(s) closed.	貨艙／液貨艙開口已關閉
Openings in superstructure closed.	船艛開口已關閉
Openings in accommodation closed.	住艙開口已關閉
Openings in...space closed.	……艙間之開口已關閉
Openings in...not accessible.	……之開口不能接近
滅火指令	
Start fire fighting.	開始滅火

Take one/two/...ire party(s) to scene.	帶一班／二班／……消防班至現場
Take one/two/...rescue team(s) to scene.	帶一組／二組／……救援組至現場
Go following route:...	經由以下路徑
Go through engine room.	仔細檢視機艙
Go through No....hold(s)/tank(s).	仔細檢視第……貨艙／液貨艙
Go through superstructure.	仔細檢視船艛
Go through accommodation.	仔細檢視住艙
Go through...space.	仔細檢視……艙間
Go through manhole(s) to...space(s).	仔細檢視人孔至……艙間
Go through funnel.	仔細檢視煙囪
Go through...	仔細檢視……
Go from outside/inside to...	從外／內行走到……
Go from port side/starboard side to...	從左舷／右舷行走到……
Go from...to...	從……行走到……
Take following (additional) safety measures and report.	採取以下（追加）安全措施，並回報
Number of members in fire party/rescue team/first aid team:...	消防班／救援組／急救組的人數為……
Have lifeline between each other/to outside.	救生索繫在每人之間／接到外部
Fire party/... team members have life lines to each other.	消防班／……組救生索繫在每人之間
Fire party/... team has lifelines to outside.	消防班／……組救生索接到外部
Have rescue team on stand by.	請救援組備便
Rescue team standing by.	救援組正在備便
Maintain visual contact.	維持目視連絡
Fire party/... team members maintain visual contact with lamps.	消防班／……組人員以號燈維持目視連絡
Maintain radio contact on VHF channel 15/17.	維持在VHF（特高頻）頻道15／17以無線電連絡
Fire party must have following outfit:...	消防班必須有以下裝備
Fire party must have protective clothing.	消防班必須有防護服

Fire party must have smoke helmets.	消防班必須有防煙頭盔
Fire party must have breathing apparatus.	消防班必須有呼吸器
Fire party must have...	消防班必須有……
Manning of fire party...teams is as follows:...	消防班／……組的編制如下
Chief Officer/Chief Engineer/...in command of fire party (No....)/...team.	大副／輪機長／……指揮（第……班／組）消防班／……組
Following officer(s)/crew member(s) in the fire party (No....)/...team:...	以下甲級船員／船員在（第……班／組）消防班／……組：……
Restrict action (in.../on...) to...minutes.	（在……／……上）的行動時間限制……分鐘內
Agree on retreat signal and report.	同意歸隊信號，並回報
Retreat signal for fire party/... team, is ... on telephone/radio.	消防班／……組之歸隊信號，以電話／無線電發出……
Visual retreat signal for fire party/...team, is ... with lamp/hand/...	消防班／……組之目視歸隊信號，是以燈／手勢／……發出……
Acoustic retreat signal for fire party/...team is ... with signal whistle/ship's whistle/...	消防班／……組之音響歸隊信號，是以號笛／汽笛／……發出……
Retreat signal for fire party/...team, is pulling lifeline...times.	滅火班撤退信號，是以拉扯救生索……次
Use the following extinguishing means…	使用以下滅火方法……
Use water in...	在……使用水
Use foam in...	在……使用泡沫
Use powder in...	在……使用粉末
Use CO_2/gas in...	在……使用CO_2／氣體
Use sand in...	在……使用沙
Use blankets for the fire in...	在……使用防火毯撲火
Use...in...(position).	在……（位置）使用……
Fire party (No....) using...in...	（第……班）消防班在……用……
Run out fire hoses.	釋放水龍帶
Fire hoses are run out.	水龍帶已放出
Water on.	打開水源
Water is on.	水源已打開

Water not on.	水源未打開
Cool down boundaries with water and report.	用水冷卻周圍，並回報
Cool down bulkheads to engine room with water.	用水冷卻機艙艙壁
Cool down bulkheads to No....hold(s)/tank(s) with water.	用水冷卻第……貨艙／液貨艙艙壁
Cool down bulkheads to accommodation with water.	用水冷卻住艙艙壁
Cool down bulkheads to...compartment with water.	用水冷卻……艙區艙壁
Cool down bulkheads to...space with water.	用水冷卻……艙間艙壁
Cool down superstructure with water.	用水冷卻船艛
Cool down...deck in area...with water.	用水冷卻……區之……甲板
Cool down room(s) below/above/next to...space/area with water.	用水冷卻在……艙間／區之上／下／旁之房間
Cool down outside plating in... area with water.	用水冷卻在……區外板
Cool down...with water.	用水冷卻……
...cooled down.	……已冷卻
解除火警	
Is fire extinguished ?	火災是否已撲滅？
Yes, fire (in...) extinguished.	是，（在……）火勢已撲滅
No, fire (in...) not extinguished (yet).	不，（在……）火勢（尚）未撲滅
Is fire under control?	火勢是否控制住？
Yes, fire (in...) under control.	是，（在……）火勢已控制
No, fire (in...) not under control (yet).	不，（在……）火勢（尚）未控制住。
Fire restricted to...space/area.	火勢已侷限於……艙間／艙區
Post fire watches and report.	請布署消防警戒，並回報
Fire watches posted (in...space/area).	（在……艙間／艙區）消防警戒已布置
Have fire patrols in...space/area.	在……艙間／區內施行消防巡邏
Have fire patrols on deck.	在甲板上施行消防巡邏

Everything in order?	每件事都妥當了嗎？
Yes, everything in order.	是，每件事都妥當了
No, following not in order...	不，以下情況不佳……
消防系統檢查	
Check fire/smoke alarms and report.	檢查火災／煙霧警報，並回報
Fire/Smoke alarms operational.	火災／煙霧警報作動正常
Fire/Smoke alarm(s) in...not operational (yet).	在……之火災／煙霧警報（尚）不能作動
Fire/Smoke alarm(s) in...operational in...minutes.	火災／煙霧警報在……分鐘內作動正常
Switch on/off fire/smoke alarms.	開／關火災／煙霧警報
Switch on/off fire/smoke alarms in all spaces.	開／關所有艙間火災／煙霧警報
Switch on/off fire/smoke alarms in engine room.	開／關在機艙內的火災／煙霧警報
Switch on/off fire/smoke alarms in cargo hold(s)/tank(s).	開／關在貨艙／液貨艙的火災／煙霧警報
Switch on/off fire/smoke alarms in superstructure.	開／關在船艛的火災／煙霧警報
Switch on/off fire/smoke alarms in accommodation.	開／關在住艙的火災／煙霧警報
Switch on/off fire/smoke alarms in ... compartment.	開／關在……艙區的火災／煙霧警報
Switch on/off fire/smoke alarm in...	開／關在……內的火災／煙霧警報
Fire/smoke alarms in...switched on/off.	在……內的火災／煙霧警報已開／關
Check fire alarm/smoke alarm displays on bridge and report.	檢查駕駛台的火災／煙霧警報顯示盤，並回報
Fire alarm/smoke alarm displays on bridge operational.	駕駛台的火災／煙霧警報顯示盤作動正常
Fire alarm/smoke alarm display(s) of...not operational (yet).	駕駛台的火災／煙霧警報顯示盤不能作動
Fire alarm/smoke alarm display(s) of... operational in ... minutes.	駕駛台的火災／煙霧警報顯示盤在……分鐘內作動正常
Check portable extinguishers and report.	檢查手提滅火器，並回報
Portable extinguishers in position and operational.	手提滅火器就位，並可使用

Portable extinguisher(s) in...not in position (yet).	在……的手提滅火器（尚）未定位
Portable extinguisher(s) in...in position in... minutes.	在……的手提滅火器在……分鐘內定位
Portable extinguisher(s) in...not accessible (yet).	在……的手提滅火器（尚）不易取得
Portable extinguisher(s) in...accessible in...minutes.	在……的手提滅火器在……分鐘內可取得
Portable extinguisher(s) in...missing.	在……的手提滅火器不見了
Replace missing portable extinguisher(s).	補充不見的手提滅火器
Seal(s) of portable extinguisher(s) in...broken.	在……的手提滅火器封條破損
Replace portable extinguisher(s) with broken seals.	更換封條破損的手提滅火器
Test certificate(s) of portable extinguisher(s) in...expired.	在……的手提滅火器之檢查證書過期
Replace expired portable extinguisher(s).	更換過期手提滅火器
Check fire mains and report.	檢查消防總管，並回報
Fire mains operational.	消防總管可使用
Hydrant(s) in...not operational (yet).	在……的消防栓（尚）不可使用
Hydrant(s) operational in ... minutes.	在……分鐘內消防栓可使用
Hydrant(s) in...not accessible (yet).	在……的消防栓（尚）不易接近
Hydrant(s) in...accessible in ... minutes.	在……分鐘內消防栓可接近
Hose(s) to hydrant(s) in...worn/cut.	在……的消防皮龍磨損／斷裂
Replace worn/cut hose(s).	更換磨損／斷裂皮龍
Hose(s) to hydrant(s) in...missing.	在……的消防皮龍不見了
Replace missing hose(s).	補充不見的皮龍
Spanner(s) to hydrant(s) in...missing.	在……的消防栓用扳手不見了
Replace missing spanner(s).	補充不見的扳手
Nozzle(s) to...not operational (yet).	在……的噴嘴（尚）不可使用
Nozzle(s) to...operational in ... minutes.	在……的噴嘴在……分鐘內可使用
Nozzle(s) to...do/does not fit.	在……的噴嘴合適／不合適
Replace nozzle(s) to...(by fitting ones).	（以合適者）更換……的噴嘴
Nozzle(s) to...missing.	在……的噴嘴不見了
Replace missing nozzle(s).	補充不見的噴嘴

Fire pump(s) in...not operational (yet).	在……的消防泵（尚）不能作動
Fire pump(s) in…operational in...minutes.	在……的消防泵……分鐘內可作動
Water pipe(s) in...leaking.	在……的水管漏水
Repair leaking water pipe(s) in...	修理……的漏水水管
Water pipe(s)...blocked.	在……的水管堵塞
Free blocked water pipe(s) in…	清通……的堵塞水管
Pressurein water pipe(s) in...too high.	在……的水管壓力太高
Reduce pressure in water pipe(s) in....	降低……水管壓力
Pressure in water pipe(s) in...too low.	在……的水管壓力太低
Increase pressure in waterpipe(s) in....	增加……的水管壓力
Check fixed foam/gas fire extinguishing system and report.	檢查固定泡沫／氣體滅火系統，並回報
Fixed foam/gas system operational.	固定泡沫／氣體系統可使用
Fixed foam/gas system not operational (yet).	固定泡沫／氣體系統（尚）不可使用
Fixed foam/gas system operational in...minutes.	固定泡沫／氣體系統在……分鐘內可使用
Check sprinkler system and report.	檢查灑水系統，並回報
Sprinkler system operational.	灑水系統可作動
Sprinkler system in...not operational (yet).	在……的灑水系統（尚）不能作動
Sprinkler system in…operational in…minutes.	在……的灑水系統……分鐘內可作動
Check ventilation system and report.	檢查通風系統，並回報
Ventilation system operational.	通風系統可作動
Ventilation system not operational (yet).	通風系統（尚）不能作動
Ventilation system will be operational in…minutes.	通風系統在……分鐘內可作動
Remote control not operational (yet).	遙控（尚）不能作動
Remote control operational in...minutes.	在……分鐘內遙控可作動
Indicators not operational (yet).	指示器（尚）不能作動
Indicators operational in...minutes.	在……分鐘內指示器可作動
Dampers in...not operational (yet).	在……擋風板（尚）不能作動
Dampers in...operational in...minutes.	在……擋風板……分鐘內可作動

221

Check skylights/windows/...and report.	檢查天窗／窗戶／……，並回報
Skylights/windows/...in/to open.	在／至……天窗／窗戶／……開著
檢查電器	
Check lighting and report.	檢查照明並回報
Lighting operational.	照明可使用
Lighting in...not operatiopal.	在……的照明不能使用
Black-out short circuitin...	在……的電跳脫／短路
Lighting operational in...minute.	在……的照明……分鐘內可使用
Switch on/off lighting in…	開／關在……的照明
Lighting in…switched on/off.	在……的照明已開／關
Check emergency power supply and report	檢查緊急電源並回報
Emergency power supply operational.	緊急電源可使用
Emergency power supply not operational.	緊急電源不能使用
Emergency power supply operational in... minutes.	緊急電源在……分鐘內可使用
Check firemen outfit and report.	檢查消防員裝具，並回報
Firemen outfits complete and available.	消防員裝具完整，並可取得
Comeplete firemen's outfits.	消防員裝具完整
Breathing apparatus (BA)/smoke helmets/safety lamps/not operational/missing.	呼吸器／防煙頭盔／安全燈／不能使用／不見了
Replace breathing apparatus/smoke helmets/safety lamps.	更換呼吸器／防煙頭頭盔／安全燈
Testcertificate(s) of...expired.	……的檢驗證明過期了
滅火及演習報告	
Fire on board!	船上失火了！
Smoke/Fire/Explosion in engine room.	機艙內發生煙／火／爆炸
Smoke/Fire/Explosionin No....cargo hold(s)/cargo tank(s).	第……號貨艙／液貨艙內發生煙／火／爆炸
Smoke/Fire/Explosion in supersucture.	船艛艙內發生煙／火／爆炸
Smoke/Fire/Explosion in accommodation.	住艙內發生煙／火／爆炸
Smoke/Fire/Explosion in...space/area.	在……區發生煙／火／爆炸
Smoke/Fire/Explosion on deck.	甲板上發生煙／火／爆炸

Smoke from ventilator(s).	通風管有煙冒出
Burning smell in...from...	……內有燒焦味／從……有焦味出來
Report injured persons...	報告受傷人員……
No person injured.	無人員受傷
Number of injuries persons/casualties...	受傷人數／受難人數……
What is on fire?	什麼著火了？
Fuel on fire.	燃油著火
Cargo on fire.	貨物著火
...on fire.	……著火
Car(s)/Truck(s)/Wagon(s) on fire.	汽車／卡車／休旅車起火
Containers (with dangerous goods) on fire.	（有危險品）貨櫃著火
No information.	不清楚
Is smoke toxic?	煙有毒嗎？
No, smoke not toxic.	沒有，煙無毒
Yes, smoke toxic.	有，煙有毒
Is fire under control?	火勢控制住了嗎？
Yes, fire in... under control.	是，在……的火勢已控制住
No, fire in...not under control (yet).	不，在……的火勢未控制住
No, fire spreading to...	不，火勢正擴散至……
No, fire (in...) not accessible.	不，（在……）的火勢不可接近
What is damage?	有何種損壞？
No damage.	無損壞
Minor/Serious or damage in...	在……有輕微／嚴重損壞
No power supply in...	在……無電可用
Pressure on fire mains.	消防總管的壓力……
Fire mains under pressure.	消防總管承受壓力……
Shut down main engine(s)/auxiliary engine(s).	關閉主機／輔引擎
Main engine(s)/Auxiliary engine(s) shut down.	主機／輪機已關閉
Stop fuel.	停住燃油
Fuel stopped.	燃油已停住

223

輪機英文

Close hatch covers.	關閉艙口蓋
Hatch covers closed.	艙口蓋已關
Close damper(s) (in…).	關閉（在……）的防火檔板
Damper(s) (in...)closed.	（在……）的防火檔板已關
Close all openings.	關閉所有開口
All openings closed.	所有關口已關閉
Switch off ventilator(s) (in...).	關閉（在……）的通風筒（管）
Ventilator(s) (in...) switched off.	（在……）的通風筒（管）已關
Tum bow/stem to windward.	轉向使艏／艉對著上風
Bow/stem turned to windward.	艏／艉轉對著上風
Tum port side/starboard side to windward.	轉向使左／右舷對著上風
Port side/Starboard side turned to windward.	左／右舷已轉對著上風
Alter course to...	變更航向為……
Course altered to...	航向改為……
液態貨物、燃油及壓艙水之操控——防止污染	
Preparing safety measures.	準備安全措施
Plug scuppers and report.	塞住排水孔，並報告
Scuppers plugged.	排水孔已塞住
Plug save-alls/drip-trays and report.	塞洩漏盤／防滴盤，並報告
Save-alls/drip-trays plugged.	洩漏盤／防滴盤已塞往
Close sea-valves/discharges and report.	關閉海底閥／出口，並報告
Sea-valves/discharges closed.	海底閥／出口已關閉
Stand by absorbent material/sand and report.	備便吸收材／沙，並報告
Absorbent material/sand standing by.	吸收材／沙已備便
Stand by spill control gear and report.	備便洩漏管制裝置，並報告
Spill control gear standing by.	洩漏管制裝置正在備便
Stand by emergency fire pump/foam monitor and report.	備便應急消防泵（幫浦）／泡沫射出器，並報告
Emergency fire pump/foam monitor standing by.	應急消防泵（幫浦）／泡沫射出器正在備便

224

Stand by fire extinguishers and report.	備便滅火器，並報告
Fire extinguishers standing by.	滅火器正在備便
Fit bonding wire and report.	安裝接地導線，並報告
Bonding wire fitted.	接地導線已安裝
Maintain contact on VHF channels...with bunker barge/oil terminal.	以 VHF （特高頻）頻道……與油駁／裝卸油站維持連絡。
溢油事故的應變	
Is oil spill plan available?	有無防止溢油計畫
Yes, oil spill plan available.	是，有防止溢油計畫
No, oil spill plan not available (yet).	不，（尚）未有防止溢油計畫
Oil spill plan available in...minutes.	防止溢油計畫在……分鐘內完成
Instruct pumpman/...and report.	向泵（幫浦）匠／……說明，並報告
Pumpman/...instructed.	已向泵（幫浦）匠說明
Operating pumping equipment.	操作泵送設備
What is (maximum) loading rate/discharge rate?	最大裝油／卸駁速率如何？
(Maximum) loading rate/discharge rate: ...tonnes per hour.	最大裝油／卸駁速率：每小時……噸
How many tonnes of...oil/...can you take?	貴船能容納……噸之……油／……？
We can take...tonnes of oil/...	本船能容納……噸之……油／……
Is COW-system/inert gas system operational?	原油洗艙系統／惰性氣體系統可操作嗎？
Yes, COW-system/inert gas system operational.	是，原油洗艙系統／惰性氣體系統可操作
No, COW-system/inert gas system not operational (yet).	不，原油洗艙系統／惰性氣體系統（尚）不可操作
COW-system/inert gas system operational in... minutes.	原油洗艙系統／惰性氣體系統在……分鐘內可操作
When will crude oil washing start?	原油洗艙將於何時開始？
Crude oil washing will start in...minutes.	原油洗艙在……分鐘內將開始
How many pumps?	有多少台泵？
Number of pumps: ...	泵數為……

What is pumping pressure?	泵壓力如何？
Pumping pressure ...bars.	泵壓力為……巴
Can we connect loading arm?	本船能連接裝貨油（液貨）懸臂嗎？
Yes, you can connect loading arm.	是，貴船能連接裝貨油（液貨）懸臂
No, you cannot connect loading arm (yet).	不，貴船不能連接裝貨油懸臂
Connect loading arm in...minutes.	在……分鐘內能連接裝貨油（液貨）懸臂
Inform minutes before loading/discharge will start/finish.	在裝貨／卸貨前……分鐘通知將開始／完成
Loading/Discharge will start/finish in...minutes.	裝貨／卸貨將在……分鐘內開始／完成
What is back pressure for stripping?	抽殘油之背壓多少？
Back pressure for stripping...bars.	抽殘油之背壓為……巴
Are cargo hoses/booms connected?	貨油軟管／吊桿連接了嗎？
Yes, cargo hoses/booms connected.	是，貨油軟管／吊桿已連接
No, cargo hoses/booms connected (yet).	不，貨油軟管／吊桿（尚）未連接
Cargo hoses/Booms connected in...minutes.	貨油軟管／吊桿在……分鐘內連接
Are cargo hoses/booms disconnected?	貨油軟管／吊桿拆開了嗎？
Yes, cargo hoses/booms disconnected.	是，貨油軟管／吊桿已拆開
No, cargo hoses/booms not disconnected (yet).	不，貨油軟管／吊桿（尚）未拆開
Cargo hoses/booms disconnected in ... minutes.	貨油軟管／吊桿在……分鐘內拆開
Are you ready to load/discharge?	貴船備妥裝／卸貨嗎？
Yes, ready to load/discharge.	是，已備妥裝／卸貨
No, not ready to load/discharge (yet).	不，（尚）未備妥裝／卸貨
Ready to load/discharge in ... minutes.	在……分鐘內備妥裝／卸貨
Keep safe working pressure.	保持安全工作壓力
Open valve(s) and report.	開啟閥，並回報
All full open aboard/ashore.	船上／岸上閥已全開
Close valve(s) and report.	關閉閥，並回報
All full closed aboard/ashore.	船上／岸上閥已全關
Start pumping slowly.	開始緩慢泵送

Are you pumping?	貴船在泵送中嗎？
Yes, pumping.	是，正泵送中
No, no pumping.	不，未泵送
Are you receiving?	貴船在接收中嗎？
Yes, receiving.	是，正接收中
No, not receiving.	不，未接收
Up pumping rate.	增加泵送速率
Down pumping rate.	降低泵送速率
(Quantity received) - stop pumping.	（數量已足）－停止泵送
<div align="center">報告及清理洩漏</div>	
Leak at manifold connection!	歧管接頭洩漏
Overflow at...!	在……溢出來了
Stop pumping!	停止泵送
Pumping stopped.	已停止泵送
How much spill?	洩漏了多少？
Spill about...tonne(s).	洩漏大約……噸
Clean up spill with...	以……清理洩漏
Stand by pollution fighting team.	防污組備便
Pollution fighting team standing by.	防污組正在備便
All crew assist to clean up spill.	所有船員協助清理洩漏
Spillage stopped.	已停止洩漏
Spill cleaned up.	已清理洩漏
Oil...escaping into water!	……油流入海中
Inform pollution control and report.	通知污染管制中心，並回報
Pollution control informed.	污染管制中心已通知
<div align="center">壓載操控</div>	
Plug scuppers and report.	塞住排水孔，並回報
Scuppers plugged.	排水孔塞住
Open sea suction valve and report.	打開海水吸入閥，並回報
Sea suction valve open.	海水吸入閥已打開

227

輪機英文

Open ballast tank valve No....and report.	打開第……壓載艙閥，並回報
Ballast tank valve No....open.	第……壓載艙閥已打開
Start ballast pump and report.	啟動壓載艙泵（幫浦），並回報
Ballast pump started.	壓載艙泵（幫浦）已啟動
Stop ballast pump and report	停止壓載艙泵（幫浦），並回報
Stop ballast pump - ballast overflow!	停止壓載艙泵（幫浦）－壓艙水滿溢！
Ballast pump stopped.	壓載艙泵（幫浦）已停
Close ballast tank valve No....and report.	關閉第……壓載艙閥，並回報
Ballast tank, valve No....closed.	第……壓載艙閥已關閉
Close sea suction valve and report.	關閉海水吸入閥，並回報
Sea suction valve closed.	海水吸入閥已關閉
Pump out ballast tank No....and report	泵出第……壓載艙，並回報
Ballast tank No....pumped out.	第……壓載艙已泵出
Stop ballast pump - ballast dirty!	停止壓載艙泵，壓艙水不乾淨！
No stripping of ballast tanks in port.	港內不可抽乾壓載艙水
清洗油艙	
Pump slops into slop tank and report.	泵污油水入污油水艙，並回報
Slops pumped into slop tank.	污水已泵入污油水艙
Dispose sludge into sludge tank and report.	將殘油泥駁入油泥艙中，並回報
Sludge disposed into sludge tank.	殘油泥已駁入殘油泥艙
Order shore slop tank/slop barge and report.	安排岸上污油水駁船，並回報
We have ... tonnes of slops/sludge.	本船有……噸污油水／油泥
Shore slop tank/slop barge ordered.	已安排岸上污油水駁船
Start pumping slops and report.	開始泵送污油水，並回報
Pumping slops started.	已開始至泵送污油水
Keep safe working pressure.	維持安全工作壓力
Stop pumping slops and report.	停止泵送污油水，並回報
Pumping slops stopped.	已停止泵送污油水

危險貨物	
Observe IMDG-Code when loading/stowing.	裝載／積載請參考 IMDG 章程
Check proper segregation of goods.	檢查貨物適當隔離
Check correct technical names in documents.	檢查文件上正確使用學名
Check correct marks/labels/placards.	檢查標記／標籤／貼示是否正確
Check compatibility of IMO-Class ... goods.	檢查IMO危險品等級……之相容性
Stow flammable goods away from engine room bulkhead/...	易燃物品儲於遠離機艙隔艙壁……之處
Stow IMO-Class...goods away from living quarters.	IMO危險品等級……貨物儲置於遠離住艙區
Stow IMO-Class...goods away from...	IMO 危險品等級……貨物遠離……
Stow IMO-Class...goods separated (by one hold) from IMO-Class...goods.	以貨艙／艙區儲置IMO危險品等級……貨物遠離IMO危險品等級……貨物
Stow infectious substances separated by one hold compartment from foodstuffs.	以貨艙／艙區儲置易傳染物質遠離食材
Stow IMO-Class...goods under deck.	儲置IMO危險品等級……貨物於甲板下
Stow IMO-Class...goods on deck.	儲置IMO危險品等級……貨物於甲板
Cover IMO-Class...goods on deck with tarpaulins.	甲板上IMO危險品等級……貨物以防水布蓋上
Stow drums away from IMO-Class...goods at minimum of metres.	將筒儲置於離開 IMO 危險品等級……貨物至少……公尺
You can stow poisonous and flammable goods in one hold.	貴船能把有毒及易燃貨物裝在同一貨艙內
Brief stevedores on dangerous goods in number hold(s).	向碼頭工人簡介第……貨艙之危險貨
Refuse damaged/wet/...packings with dangerous goods.	拒絕受損／受潮／……之裝有危險貨包裝
Ventilate hold(s) before entering.	進艙前先通風
Use calibrated test meters for checking oxygen level.	使用經校正之測試儀，量測含氧量
Load/unload IMO-Class...goods first.	先裝／卸IMO危險品等級……貨物
No smoking when loading/unloading.	裝／卸貨時，請勿吸煙

230

Sling(s) with carboys/bottles/drums/...of IMO-Class...goods dropped on deck.	裝有IMO危險品等級⋯⋯貨物之酸瓶／瓶／筒連同吊具掉落至甲板
Liquid/powder/gas escaping.	液體／粉末／氣體流失
Several drums/barrels/tanks/...leaking.	數筒／桶／槽／⋯⋯洩漏
Several drums/barrels/tanks/... deformed.	數筒／桶／槽／⋯⋯變形
...container with IMO-Class...goods leaking out of door.	裝有IMO危險品等級⋯⋯貨物之⋯⋯貨櫃，其貨洩漏出門外
洩漏物質使貨物受損	
Leaking substances/oil/liquid/... of IMO-Class...escaped into sea (inform pollution control).	IMO危險品等級⋯⋯之洩漏物質／油／液體流入海中（通知污染管制中心）
Leaking substances/oil/liquid/...of IMO-Class...escaped into harbour basin (inform pollution control).	IMO危險品等級⋯⋯之洩漏物質／油／液體流入港區（通知污染管制中心）
Temperature in locker/container/...with IMO-Class...goods increasing (rapidly).	貯藏室／貨櫃／⋯⋯內IMO危險品等級⋯⋯貨物之溫度（快速）上升
Orange/red/white/...smoke developing among IMO-Class...goods (on deck).	（甲板上）IMO 危險品等級⋯⋯油貨物產生橘紅色／紅色／白色／⋯⋯之煙霧
(Minor) explosion in number...hold.	在第⋯⋯貨艙內發生輕微爆炸
Minor/Major damage to gas tank/container/...	瓦斯槽／容器／⋯⋯發生輕微／嚴重損壞
Minor/Major fire was in number...hold.	在第⋯⋯貨艙內發生輕微／嚴重火災

家圖書館出版品預行編目資料

輪機英文 = English for marine enginee／
華健編著. ――初二版. ――臺北市：五南
圖書出版股份有限公司, 2025.01
面；　公分
SBN 978-626-423-040-7 (平裝)

.CST: 英語　2.CST: 輪機工程　3.CST: 讀本

05.18　　　　　　　　113019272

5A02

輪機英文

作　　者 ― 華　健 (498)

編輯主編 ― 王正華

責任編輯 ― 張維文

封面設計 ― 姚孝慈

出 版 者 ― 五南圖書出版股份有限公司

發 行 人 ― 楊榮川

總 經 理 ― 楊士清

總 編 輯 ― 楊秀麗

地　　址：106臺北市大安區和平東路二段339號4樓

電　　話：(02)2705-5066　　傳　　真：(02)2706-6100

網　　址：https://www.wunan.com.tw

電子郵件：wunan@wunan.com.tw

劃撥帳號：01068953

戶　　名：五南圖書出版股份有限公司

法律顧問　林勝安律師

出版日期　2017年8月初版一刷（共三刷）
　　　　　2025年1月二版一刷

定　　價　新臺幣380元

經典永恆・名著常在

五十週年的獻禮——經典名著文庫

五南，五十年了，半個世紀，人生旅程的一大半，走過來了。

思索著，邁向百年的未來歷程，能為知識界、文化學術界作些什麼？

在速食文化的生態下，有什麼值得讓人雋永品味的？

歷代經典・當今名著，經過時間的洗禮，千錘百鍊，流傳至今，光芒耀人；

不僅使我們能領悟前人的智慧，同時也增深加廣我們思考的深度與視野。

我們決心投入巨資，有計畫的系統梳選，成立「經典名著文庫」，

希望收入古今中外思想性的、充滿睿智與獨見的經典、名著。

這是一項理想性的、永續性的巨大出版工程。

不在意讀者的眾寡，只考慮它的學術價值，力求完整展現先哲思想的軌跡；

為知識界開啟一片智慧之窗，營造一座百花綻放的世界文明公園，

任君遨遊、取菁吸蜜、嘉惠學子！